A. Merritt

Burn Witch Burn!

Futura Publications Limited
An Orbit Book

An Orbit Book

First published in Great Britain in 1934

First Orbit edition published in 1974
by Futura Publications Limited
49 Poland Street,
London W1A 2LG

ISBN 0 8600 7811 6
Printed in Great Britain by
Hazell Watson & Viney Ltd
Aylesbury, Bucks

Futura Publications Limited
49 Poland Street,
London W1A 2LG

Abraham Merritt was born in 1884 in New Jersey, U.S.A., into an old Quaker family. He was related through his maternal grandmother to Fenimore Cooper. His father was an architect. When he was ten, the family moved to Philadelphia. He began reading law but soon decided to become a journalist instead. His apprenticeship was cut short when he became involved, as a potential witness, in a politically charged trial. He was rapidly shipped off to Mexico and other points south where writs of extradition did not run.

Eventually he returned to the States and became a reporter on the *Philadelphia Inquirer*, specialising in murders, mysteries and the investigation of shady politics. In 1912 he moved to *The American Weekly*, which was the Sunday supplement of the Hearst newspapers. When the Editor died suddenly in 1937, Merritt succeeded him. He wrote a number of novels and short stories but was never prolific, for the work of editing left little time for his own writing.

His interests, stimulated by personal observation in the Pennsylvania Dutch region and among the Mayan ruins of Latin America, were in folk-lore, the survival of strange old practices and the relics of ancient civilizations. He wove them into tales – 'The Moon Pool', 'Dwellers in the Mirage', 'Seven Footprints to Satan' and 'Burn Witch Burn!' – which were immediately recognised as deserving a place in the very first rank of imaginative fiction.

He died in 1943.

Also by Abraham Merritt

FOREWORD

I am a medical man specializing in neurology and diseases of the brain. My peculiar field is abnormal psychology, and in it I am recognized as an expert. I am closely connected with two of the foremost hospitals in New York, and have received many honors in this country and abroad. I set this down, risking identification, not through egotism but because I desire to show that I was competent to observe, and competent to bring practiced scientific judgment upon, the singular events I am about to relate.

I say that I risk identification, because Lowell is not my name. It is a pseudonym, as are the names of all the other characters in this narrative. The reasons for this evasion will become increasingly apparent.

Yet I have the strongest feeling that the facts and observations which in my case-books are grouped under the heading of 'The Dolls of Mme. Mandilip' should be clarified, set down in orderly sequence and be made known. Obviously, I could do this in the form of a report to one of my medical societies, but I am too well aware of the way my colleagues would receive such a paper, and with what suspicion, pity or even abhorrence, they would henceforth regard me – so counter to accepted notions of cause and effect do many of these facts and observations run.

But now, orthodox man of medicine that I am, I ask myself whether there may not be causes other than those we admit. Forces and energies which we stubbornly disavow because we can find no explanation for

5

them within the narrow confines of our present knowledge. Energies whose reality is recognized in folk-lore, the ancient traditions, of all peoples, and which, to justify our ignorance, we label myth and superstition.

A wisdom, a science, immeasurably old. Born before history, but never dying nor ever wholly lost. A secret wisdom, but always with its priests and priestesses guarding its dark flame, passing it on from century to century. Dark flame of forbidden knowledge . . . burning in Egypt before ever the Pyramids were raised; and in temples crumbling now beneath the Gobi's sands; known to the sons of Ad whom Allah, so say the Arabs, turned to stone for their sorceries ten thousand years before Abraham trod the streets of Ur of the Chaldees; known in China – and known to the Tibetan lama, the Buryat shamen of the steppes and to the warlock of the South Seas alike.

Dark flame of evil wisdom . . . deepening the shadows of Stonehenge's brooding menhirs; fed later by hands of Roman legionaries; gathering strength, none knows why, in medieval Europe . . . and still burning, still alive, still strong.

Enough of preamble. I begin where the dark wisdom, if that it were, first cast its shadow upon me.

CONTENTS

CHAPTER ONE

The Unknown Death

I heard the clock strike one as I walked up the hospital steps. Ordinarily I would have been in bed and asleep, but there was a case in which I was much interested, and Braile, my assistant, had telephoned me of certain developments which I wished to observe. It was a night in early November. I paused for a moment at the top of the steps to look at the brilliancy of the stars. As I did so, an automobile drew up at the entrance to the hospital.

As I stood, wondering what its arrival at that hour meant, a man slipped out of it. He looked sharply up and down the deserted street, then threw the door wide open. Another man emerged. The two of them stooped and seemed to be fumbling around inside. They straightened and then I saw that they had locked their arms around the shoulders of a third. They moved forward, not supporting but carrying this other man. His head hung upon his breast and his body swung limply.

A fourth man stepped from the automobile.

I recognized him. He was Julian Ricori, a notorious underworld chieftain, one of the finished products of the Prohibition Law. He had been pointed out to me several times. Even if he had not been, the newspapers would have made me familiar with his features and figure. Lean and long, with silvery white hair, always immaculately dressed, a leisured type from outward seeming, rather than leader of such activities as those of which he was accused.

I had been standing in the shadow, unnoticed. I stepped out of the shadow. Instantly the burdened pair halted, swiftly as hunting hounds. Their free hands dropped into the pockets of their coats. Menace was in that movement.

'I am Dr. Lowell,' I said, hastily. 'Connected with the hospital. Come right along.'

They did not answer me. Nor did their gaze waver from me; nor did they move. Ricori stepped in front of them. His hands were also in his pockets. He looked me over, then nodded to the others; I felt the tension relax.

'I know you, Doctor,' he said pleasantly, in oddly precise English. 'But that was quite a chance you took. If I might advise you, it is not well to move so quickly when those come whom you do not know, and at night – not in this town.'

'But,' I said, 'I do know you, Mr. Ricori.'

'Then,' he smiled, faintly, 'your judgment was doubly at fault. And my advice doubly pertinent.'

There was an awkward moment of silence. He broke it.

'And being who I am, I shall feel much better inside your doors than outside.'

I opened the doors. The two men passed through with their burden, and after them Ricori and I. Once within, I gave way to my professional instincts and stepped up to the man the two were carrying. They shot a quick glance at Ricori. He nodded. I raised the man's head.

A little shock went through me. The man's eyes were wide open. He was neither dead nor unconscious. But upon his face was the most extraordinary expression of terror I had ever seen in a long experience with sane, insane and borderline cases. It was not undiluted fear.

It was mixed with an equally disturbing horror. The eyes, blue and with distended pupils, were like exclamation points to the emotions printed upon that face. They stared up at me, through me and beyond me. And still they seemed to be looking inward – as though whatever nightmare vision they were seeing was both behind and in front of them.

'Exactly!' Ricori had been watching me closely. 'Exactly, Dr. Lowell, what could it be that my friend has seen – or has been given – that could make him appear so? I am most anxious to learn. I am willing to spend much money to learn. I wish him cured, yes – but I shall be frank with you, Dr. Lowell. I would give my last penny for the certainty that those who did this to him could not do the same thing to me – could not make me as he is, could not make me see what he is seeing, could not make feel what he is feeling.'

At my signal, orderlies had come up. They took the patient and laid him on a stretcher. By this time the resident physician had appeared. Ricori touched my elbow.

'I know a great deal about you, Dr. Lowell,' he said. 'I would like you to take full charge of this case.'

I hesitated.

He continued, earnestly: 'Could you drop everything else? Spend all your time upon it? Bring in any others you wish to consult – don't think of expense—'

'A moment, Mr. Ricori,' I broke in. 'I have patients who cannot be neglected. I will give all the time I can spare, and so will my assistant, Dr. Braile. Your friend will be constantly under observation here by people who have my complete confidence. Do you wish me to take the case under those conditions?'

He acquiesced, though I could see he was not entirely

satisfied. I had the patient taken to an isolated private room, and went through the necessary hospital formalities. Ricori gave the man's name as Thomas Peters, asserted that he knew of no close relations, had himself recorded as Peters' nearest friend, assumed all responsibility, and taking out a roll of currency, skimmed a thousand-dollar bill from it, passing it to the desk as 'preliminary costs.'

I asked Ricori if he would like to be present at my examination. He said that he would. He spoke to his two men, and they took positions at each side of the hospital doors – on guard. Ricori and I went to the room assigned to the patient. The orderlies had stripped him, and he lay upon the adjustable cot, covered by a sheet. Braile, for whom I had sent, was bending over Peters, intent upon his face, and plainly puzzled. I saw with satisfaction that Nurse Walters, an unusually capable and conscientious young woman had been assigned to the case. Braile looked up at me. He said:

'Obviously some drug.'

'Maybe,' I answered. 'But if so – then a drug I have never encountered. Look at his eyes—'

I closed Peters' lids. As soon as I had lifted my fingers they began to rise, slowly, until they were again wide open. Several times I tried to shut them. Always they opened: the terror, the horror in them, undiminished.

I began my examination. The entire body was limp, muscle and joints. It was as flaccid, the simile came to me, as a doll. It was as though every motor nerve had gone out of business. Yet there was none of the familiar symptoms of paralysis. Nor did the body respond to any sensory stimulus, although I struck down into the nerve trunks. The only reaction I could obtain was a slight contraction of the dilated pupils under strongest light.

Hoskins, the pathologist, came in to take his samples for blood tests. When he had drawn what he wanted, I went over the body minutely. I could find not a single puncture, wound or abrasion. Peters was hairy. With Ricori's permission, I had him shaved clean – chest, shoulders, legs, even the head. I found nothing to indicate that a drug might have been given him by hypodermic. I had the stomach emptied and took specimens from the excretory organs, including the skin. I examined the membranes of nose and throat : they seemed healthy and normal; nevertheless, I had smears taken from them. The blood pressure was low, the temperature slightly subnormal; but that might mean nothing I gave an injection of adrenalin. There was absolutely no reaction from it. That might mean much.

'Poor devil,' I said to myself. 'I'm going to try to kill that nightmare for you, at any rate.'

I gave him a minimum hypo of morphine. It might have been water for all the good it did. Then I gave him all I dared. His eyes remained open, terror and horror undiminished. And pulse and respiration unchanged.

Ricori had watched all these operations with intense interest. I had done all I could for the time, and told him so.

'I can do no more,' I said, 'until I receive the reports of the specimens. Frankly, I am all at sea. I know of no disease nor drug which would produce these conditions.'

'But Dr. Braile,' he said, 'mentioned a drug—'

'A suggestion only,' interposed Braile hastily. 'Like Dr. Lowell, I know of no drug which would cause such symptoms.'

13

Ricori glanced at Peters' face and shivered.

'Now,' I said, 'I must ask you some questions. Has this man been ill? If so, has he been under medical care? If he has not actually been ill, has he spoken of any discomfort? Or have you noticed anything unusual in his manner or behaviour?'

'No, to all questions,' he answered. 'Peters has been in closest touch with me for the past week. He has not been ailing in the least. To-night we were talking in my apartments, eating a late and light dinner. He was in high spirits. In the middle of a word, he stopped, half-turned his head as though listening; then slipped from his chair to the floor. When I bent over him he was as you see him now. That was precisely half after midnight. I brought him here at once.'

'Well,' I said, 'that at least gives us the exact time of the seizure. There is no use of your remaining, Mr. Ricori, unless you wish.'

He studied his hands a few moments, rubbing the carefully manicured nails.

'Dr. Lowell,' he said at last, 'if this man dies without your discovering what killed him, I will pay you the customary fees and the hospital the customary charges and no more. If he dies and you make this discovery after his death, I will give a hundred thousand dollars to any charity you name. But if you make the discovery before he dies, and restore him to health – I will give you the same sum.'

We stared at him, and then as the significance of this remarkable offer sank in, I found it hard to curb my anger.

'Ricori,' I said, 'you and I live in different worlds, therefore I answer you politely, although I find it difficult. I will do all in my power to find out what is the matter with your friend and to cure him. I would do that if he and you were paupers. I am interested in him only as a problem which challenges me as a physician. But I am not interested in you in the slightest. Nor in your money. Nor in your offer. Consider it definitely rejected. Do you thoroughly understand that?'

He betrayed no resentment.

'So much so that more than ever do I wish you to take full charge,' he said.

'Very well. Now where can I get you if I want to bring you here quickly?'

'With your permission,' he answered, 'I should like to have – well, representatives in this room at all times. There will be two of them. If you want me, tell them – and I will soon be here.'

I smiled at that, but he did not.

'You have reminded me,' he said, 'that we live in different worlds. You take your precautions to go safely in your world – and I order my life to minimize the perils of mine. Not for a moment would I presume to advise you how to walk among the dangers of your laboratory, Dr. Lowell. I have the counterparts of those dangers. *Bene* – I guard against them as best I can.'

It was a most irregular request, of course. But I found myself close to liking Ricori just then, and saw clearly his point of view. He knew that and pressed the advantage.

'My men will be no bother,' he said. 'They will not interfere in any way with you. If what I suspect to be true is true – they will be a protection for you and your aids as well. But they, and those who relieve them, must stay in the room night and day. If Peters is taken from the room, they must accompany him – no matter where it is that he is taken.'

15

'I can arrange it,' I said. Then, at his request, I sent an orderly down to the doors. He returned with one of the men Ricori had left on guard. Ricori whispered to him, and he went out. In a little while two other men came up. In the meantime I had explained the peculair situation to the resident and the superintendent and secured the necessary permission for their stay.

The two men were well-dressed, polite, of a singularly tight-lipped and cold-eyed alertness. One of them shot a glance at Peters.

'Christ!' he muttered.

The room was a corner one with two windows, one opening out on the Drive, the other on the side street. Besides these, there were no other openings except the door to the hall; the private bathroom being enclosed and having no windows. Ricori and the two inspected the room minutely, keeping away, I noticed, from the windows. He asked me then if the room could be darkened. Much interested, I nodded. The lights were turned off, the three went to the windows, opened them and carefully scrutinized the six-storey sheer drop to both streets. On the side of the Drive there is nothing but the open space above the park. Opposite the other side is a church.

'It is at this side you must watch,' I heard Ricori say; he pointed to the church. 'You can turn the lights on now, Doctor.'

He stared toward the door, then turned.

'I have many enemies, Dr. Lowell. Peters was my right hand. If it was one of these enemies who struck him, he did it to weaken me. Or, perhaps, because he had not the opportunity to strike at me. I look at Peters, and for the first time in my life I, Ricori – am afraid.

16

I have no wish to be the next, I have no wish – to look into hell!'

I grunted at that! he had put so aptly what I had felt and had not formulated into words.

He started to open the door. He hesitated.

'One thing more. If there should be any telephone calls inquiring as to Peters' condition let one of these men, or their reliefs, answer. If any should come in person making inquiry, allow them to come up – but if they are more than one, let only one come at a time. If any should appear, asserting that they are relations, again let these men meet and question them.'

He gripped my hand, then opened the door of the room. Another pair of the efficient-appearing retainers were awaiting him at the threshold. They swung in before and behind him. As he walked away, I saw that he was crossing himself vigorously.

I closed the door and went back into the room. I looked down on Peters—

If I had been religious, I too would have been doing some crossing. The expression on Peters' face had changed. The terror and horror were gone. He still seemed to be looking both beyond me and into himself, but it was a look of evil expectancy – so evil that involuntarily I shot a glance over my shoulder to see what ugly thing might be creeping upon me.

There was nothing. One of Ricori's gunmen sat in the corner of the window, in the shadow, watching the parapet of the church roof opposite; the other sat stolidly at the door.

Braile and Nurse Walters were at the other side of the bed. Their eyes were fixed with horrified fascination on Peters' face. And then I saw Braile turn his head and stare about the room – as I had.

Suddenly Peters' eyes seemed to focus, to become aware of the three of us, to become aware of the entire room. They flashed with an unholy glee. That glee was not maniacal – it was diabolical. It was the look of a devil long exiled from his well-beloved hell, and suddenly summoned to return.

Or was it like the glee of some devil sent hurtling out of his hell to work his will upon whom he might?

Very well do I know how fantastic, how utterly unscientific, are such comparisons. Yet not otherwise can I describe that strange change.

Then, abruptly as the closing of a camera shutter, that expression fled and the old terror and horror came back. I gave an involuntary gasp of relief, for it was precisely as though some evil presence had withdrawn. The nurse was trembling; Baile asked, in a strained voice:

'How about another hypodermic?'

'No,' I said. 'I want you to watch the progress of this – whatever it is – without drugs. I'm going down to the laboratory. Watch him closely until I return.'

I went down to the laboratory. Hoskins looked up at me.

'Nothing wrong, so far. Remarkable health, I'd say. Of course all I've results on are the simpler tests.'

I nodded. I had an uncomfortable feeling that the other tests also would show nothing. And I had been more shaken than I would have cared to confess by those alterations of hellish fear, hellish expectancy and hellish glee in Peters' face and eyes. The whole case troubled me, gave me a nightmarish feeling of standing outside some door which it was vitally important to open, and to which not only did I have no key but couldn't find the keyhole. I have found that concentration upon microscopic work often permits me to think

18

more freely upon problems. So I took a few smears of Peters' blood and began to study them, not with any expectation of finding anything, but to slip the brakes from another part of my brain.

I was on my fourth slide when suddenly I realized that I was looking at the incredible. As I had perfunctorily moved the slide, a white corpuscle had slid into the field of vision. Only a simple white corpuscle – but within it was a spark of phosphorescence, shining out like a tiny lamp!

I thought at first that it was some effect of the light, but no manipulation of the illumination changed that spark. I rubbed my eyes and looked again. I called Hoskins.

'Tell me if you see something peculiar in there.'

He peered into the microscope. He stared, then shifted the light as I had.

'What do you see, Hoskins?'

He said, still staring through the lens:

'A leucocyte inside of which is a globe of phosphorescence. Its glow is neither dimmed when I turn on the full illumination, nor is it increased when I lessen it. In all except the ingested globe the corpuscle seems normal.'

'And all of which,' I said, 'is quite impossible.'

'Quite,' he agreed, straightening. 'Yet there it is!'

I transferred the slide to the micro-manipulator, hoping to isolate the corpuscle, and touched it with the tip of the manipulating needle. At the instant of contact the corpuscle seemed to burst. The globe of phosphorescence appeared to flatten, and something like a miniature flash of heat-lightning ran over the visible portion of the slide.

And that was all – the phosphorescence was gone.

We prepared and examined slide after slide. Twice more we found a tiny shining globe, and each time with the same result, the bursting corpuscle, the strange flicker of faint luminosity – then nothing.

The laboratory 'phone rang. Hoskins answered.

'It's Braile. He wants you – quick.'

'Keep after it, Hoskins,' I said, and hastened to Peters' room. Entering, I saw Nurse Walters, face chalk white, eyes closed, standing with her back turned to the bed. Braile was leaning over the patient, stethoscope to his heart. I looked at Peters, and stood stock still, something like a touch of unreasoning panic at my own heart. Upon his face was that look of devilish expectancy, but intensified. As I looked, it gave way to the diabolic joy, and that, too, was intensified. The face held it for not many seconds. Back came the expectancy – then on its heels the unholy glee. The two expressions altered, rapidly. They flickered over Peters' face like – like the flickers of the tiny lights within the corpuscles of his blood—

Braile spoke to me through stiff lips:

'His heart stopped three minutes ago! He ought to be dead – yet listen—'

The body of Peters stretched and stiffened. A sound came from his lips – a chuckling sound; low yet singularly penetrating, inhuman, the chuttering laughter of a devil. The gunman at the window leaped to his feet, his chair going over with a crash. The laughter choked and died away, and the body of Peters lay limp.

I heard the door open, and Ricori's voice:

'How is he, Dr. Lowell? I could not sleep—'

He saw Peters' face.

'Mother of Christ!' I heard him whisper. He dropped to his knees.

20

I saw him dimly – for I could not take my eyes from Peters' face. It was the face of a grinning, triumphant fiend – all humanity wiped from it – the face of a demon straight out of some mad medieval painter's hell. The blue eyes, now utterly malignant, glared at Ricori.

And as I looked, the dead hands moved; slowly the arms bent up from the elbows, the fingers contracting like claws; the dead body began to stir beneath the covers —

At that the spell of nightmare dropped from me; for the first time in hours I was on ground that I knew. It was the *rigor mortis*, the stiffening of death – but setting in more quickly and proceeding at a rate I had never known.

I stepped forward and drew the lids down over the glaring eyes. I covered the dreadful face.

I looked at Ricori. He was still on his knees, crossing himself and praying. And kneeling beside him, arm around his shoulders, was Nurse Walters, and she, too, was praying.

Somewhere a clock struck five.

CHAPTER TWO

The Questionnaire

I offered to go home with Ricori, and somewhat to my surprise he accepted with alacrity. The man was pitiably shaken. We rode silently, the tight-lipped gunman alert. Peters' face kept floating before me.

I gave Ricori a strong sedative, and left him sleeping, his men on guard. I had told him that I meant to make a complete autopsy.

Returning to the hospital in his car, I found the body of Peters had been taken to the mortuary. *Rigor mortis*, Braile told me, had been complete in less than an hour – an astonishingly short time. I made the necessary arrangements for the autopsy, and took Braile home with me to snatch a few hours' sleep. It is difficult to convey by words the peculiarly unpleasant impression the whole occurrence had made upon me. I can only say that I was as grateful for Braile's company as he seemed to be for mine.

When I awoke, the nightmarish oppression still lingered, though not so strongly. It was about two when we began the autopsy. I lifted the sheet from Peters' body with noticeable hesitation. I stared at his face with amazement. All diabolism had been wiped away. It was serene, unlined – the face of a man who had died peacefully, with no agony either of body or mind. I lifted his hand, it was limp, the whole body flaccid, the rigor gone.

It was then, I think, that I first felt full conviction I

was dealing with an entirely new, or at least unknown, agency of death, whether microbic or otherwise. As a rule, rigor does not set in for sixteen to twenty-four hours, depending upon the condition of the patient before death, temperature and a dozen other things. Normally, it does not disappear for forty-eight to seventy-two hours. Usually a rapid setting-in of the stiffening means as rapid a disappearance, and vice versa. Diabetics stiffen quicker than others. A sudden brain injury, like shooting, is even swifter. In this case, the rigor had begun instantaneously with death, and must have completed its cycle in the astonishingly short time of less than five hours – for the attendant told me that he had examined the body about ten o'clock and he had thought that stiffening had not yet set in. As a matter of fact, it had come and gone.

The results of the autopsy can be told in two sentences. There was no ascertainable reason why Peters should not be alive. And he was dead!

Later, when Hoskins made his reports, both of these utterly conflicting statements continued to be true. There was no reason why Peters should be dead. Yet dead he was. If the enigmatic lights we had observed had anything to do with his death, they left no traces. His organs were perfect, all else as it should have been; he was, indeed, an extraordinarily healthy specimen. Nor had Hoskins been able to capture any more of the light-carrying corpuscles after I had left him.

That night I framed a short letter describing briefly the symptoms observed in Peters' case, not dwelling upon the changes in expression but referring cautiously to 'unusual grimaces' and a 'look of intense fear.' Braile and I had this manifolded and mailed to every physician in Greater New York. I personally attended to a quiet

23

inquiry to the same effect among the hospitals. The letters asked if the physicians had treated any patients with similar symptoms, and if so to give particulars, names, addresses, occupations and any characteristic interest under seal, of course, of professional confidence. I flattered myself that my reputation was such that none of those who received the questionnaires would think the request actuated either by idle curiosity or slightest unethical motive.

I received in response seven letters and a personal visit from the writer of one of them. Each letter, except one, gave me in various degrees of medical conservatism, the information I had asked. After reading them, there was no question that within six months seven persons of oddly dissimilar characteristics and stations in life had died as had Peters.

Chronologically, the cases were as follows:

May 25: Ruth Bailey, spinster; fifty years old; moderately wealthy; Social Registerite and best of reputation; charitable and devoted to children. June 20: Patrick McIlraine; bricklayer; wife and two children. August 1: Anita Green; child of eleven; parents in moderate circumstances and well educated. August 15: Steve Standish; acrobat; thirty; wife and three children. August 30: John J. Marshall; banker; sixty; interested in child welfare. September 10: Phineas Dimott; thirty-five; trapeze performer; wife and small child. October 12: Hortense Darnley; about thirty; no occupation.

Their addresses, except two, were widely scattered throughout the city.

Each of the letters noted the sudden onset of *rigor mortis* and its rapid passing. Each of them gave the time of death following the initial seizure as approximately five hours. Five of them referred to the changing expressions which had so troubled me; in the guarded way they did it I read the bewilderment of the writers.

'Patient's eyes remained open,' recorded the physician in charge of the spinster Bailey. 'Staring, but gave no sign of recognition of surroundings and failed to focus upon or present any evidence of seeing objects held before them. Expression one of intense terror, giving away toward death to others peculiarly disquieting to observer. The latter intensified after death ensued. *Rigor mortis* complete and dissipated within five hours.'

The physician in charge of McIlraine, the bricklayer, had nothing to say about the ante-mortem phenomena, but wrote at some length about the expression of his patient's face after death.

'It had,' he reported, 'nothing in common with the muscular contraction of the so-called "Hippocratic countenance,' nor was it in any way the staring eyes and contorted mouth familiarly known as the death grin. There was no suggestion of agony, after the death – rather the opposite. I would term the expression one of unusual malice.'

The report of the physician who had attended Standish, the acrobat, was perfunctory, but it mentioned that 'after patient had apparently died, singularly disagreeable sounds emanated from his throat.' I wondered whether these had been the same demonic machinations that had come from Peters, and, if so, I could not wonder at all at my correspondent's reticence concerning them.

I knew the physician who had attended the banker – opinionated, pompous, a perfect doctor of the very rich.

'There can be no mystery as to the cause of death,' he wrote. 'It was certainly thrombosis, a clot somewhere in the brain. I attach no importance whatever to the facial grimaces, nor to the time element involved in the rigor. You know, my dear Lowell,' he added, patronizingly, 'it is an axiom in forensic medicine that one can prove anything by *rigor mortis*.'

I would have liked to have replied that when in doubt thrombosis as a diagnosis is equally as useful in covering the ignorance of practitioners, but it would not have punctured his complacency.

The Dimott report was a simple record with no comment whatever upon grimaces or sounds.

But the doctor who had attended little Anita had not been so reticent.

'The child,' he wrote, 'had been beautiful. She seemed to suffer no pain, but at the onset of the illness I was shocked by the intensity of terror in her fixed gaze. It was like a walking nightmare – for unquestionably she was conscious until death. Morphine in almost lethal dosage produced no change in this symptom, nor did it seem to have any effect upon heart or respiration. Later the terror disappeared, giving way to other emotions which I hesitate to describe in this report, but will do so in person if you so desire. The aspect of the child after death was peculiarly disturbing, but again I would rather speak than write of that.'

There was a hastily scrawled postscript; I could see him hesitating, then giving way at last to the necessity of unburdening his mind, dashing off that postscript and rushing the letter away before he could reconsider—

'I have written that the child was conscious *until death*. What haunts me is the conviction that she was

26

conscious *after physical death*! Let me talk to you.'

I nodded with satisfaction. I had not dared to put that observation down in my questionnaire. And if it has been true of the other cases, as I now believe it must have been, all the doctors except Standish's had shared my conservatism – or timidity. I called little Anita's physician upon the 'phone at once. He was strongly perturbed. In every detail his case had paralleled that of Peters. He kept repeating over and over:

'The child was sweet and good as an angel, and she changed into a devil!'

I promised to keep him apprised of any discoveries I might make, and shortly after our conversation, I was visited by the young physician who had attended Hortense Darnley. Doctor Y——, as I shall call him, had nothing to add to the medical aspect other than what I already knew, but his talk suggested the first practical line of approach toward the problem.

His office, he said, was in the apartment house which had been Hortense Darnley's home. He had been working late, and had been summoned to her apartment about ten o'clock by the woman's maid, a colored girl. He had found the patient lying upon her bed, and had at once been struck by the expression of terror on her face and the extraordinary limpness of her body. He described her as blonde, blue-eyed – 'the doll type.'

A man was in the apartment. He had at first evaded giving his name, saying that he was merely a friend. At first glance, Dr. Y—— had thought the woman had been subjected to some violence, but examination revealed no bruises or other injuries. The 'friend' had told him they had been eating dinner when 'Miss Darnley flopped right down on the floor as though all

27

her bones had gone soft, and we couldn't get anything out of her.' The maid confirmed this. There was a half-eaten dinner on the table, and both man and servant declared Hortense had been in the best of spirits. There had been no quarrel. Reluctantly, the 'friend' had admitted that the seizure had occurred three hours before, and that they had tried to 'bring her about' themselves, calling upon him only when the alternating expressions which I have referred to in the case of Peters began to appear.

As the seizure progressed, the maid had become hysterical with fright and fled. The man was of tougher timber and had remained until the end. He had been much shaken, as had Dr. Y——, by the after-death phenomena. Upon the physician declaring that the case was one for the coroner, he had lost his reticence, volunteering his name as James Martin, and expressing himself as eager for a complete autopsy. He was quite frank as to his reasons. The Darnley woman had been his mistress, and he 'had enough trouble without her death pinned to me.'

There had been a thorough autopsy. No trace of disease or poison had been found. Beyond a slight valvular trouble of the heart, Hortense Darnley had been perfectly healthy. The verdict had been death by heart disease. But Dr. Y—— was perfectly convinced the heart had nothing to do with it.

It was, of course, quite obvious that Hortense Darnley had died from the same cause or agency as had all the others. But to me the outstanding fact was that her apartment had been within a stone's throw of the address Ricori had given me as that of Peters. Furthermore, Martin was of the same world, if Dr. Y——'s impressions were correct. Here was conceivably a link between two of the cases – missing in the others. I determined to call in Ricori, to lay all the cards before him, and enlist his aid if possible.

My investigation had consumed about two weeks. During that time I had become well acquainted with Ricori. For one thing he interested me immensely as a product of present-day conditions; for another I liked him, despite his reputation. He was remarkably well read, of a high grade of totally unmoral intelligence, subtle and superstitious – in olden time he would probably have been a Captain of Condettieri, his wits and sword for hire. I wondered what were his antecedents. He had paid me several visits since the death of Peters, and quite plainly my liking was reciprocated. On these visits he was guarded by the tight-lipped man who had watched by the hospital window. This man's name, I learned, was McCann. He was Ricori's most trusted bodyguard, apparently wholly devoted to his white-haired chief. He was an interesting character too, and quite approved of me. He was a drawling Southerner who had been, as he put it, 'a cow-nurse down Arizona way, and then got too popular on the Border.'

'I'm for you, Doc,' he told me. 'You're sure good for the boss. Sort of take his mind off business. An' when I come here I can keep my hands outa my pockets. Any time anybody's cutting in on your cattle, let me know. I'll ask for a day off.'

Then he remarked casually that he 'could ring a quarter with six holes at a hundred foot range.'

I did not know whether this was meant humorously or seriously. At any rate, Ricori never went anywhere without him; and it showed me how much he had thought of Peters that he had left McCann to guard him.

29

I got in touch with Ricori and asked him to take dinner with Braile and me that night at my house. At seven he arrived, telling his chauffeur to return at ten. We sat at table, with McCann, as usual on watch in my hall, thrilling, I knew, my two night nurses – I have a small private hospital adjunct – by playing the part of a gunman as conceived by the motion pictures.

Dinner over, I dismissed the butler and came to the point. I told Ricori of my questionnaire, remarking that by it I had unearthed seven cases similar to that of Peters.

'You can dismiss from your mind any idea that Peters' death was due to his connection with you, Ricori,' I said. 'With one possible exception, none of the seven persons involved belongs to what you have called your world. If that one exception does touch your sphere of activities, it does not alter the absolute certainty that you are not involved in any way. Have you known, or ever heard of, a woman name Hortense Darnley?'

He shook his head.

'She lived,' I said, 'practically opposite the address you gave me for Peters.'

'But Peters did not live at that address,' he smiled, half-apologetically. 'You see, I did not know you then as well as now.'

That, I admit, set me back somewhat.

'Well,' I went on. 'Do you know a man named Martin?'

'Yes,' he said, 'I do. In fact I know several Martins. Can you describe the one you mean – or do you know his first name?'

'James,' I replied.

Again he shook his head, frowning.

'McCann may know,' he said at last. 'Will you call him, Dr. Lowell?'

I summoned the butler, and sent for McCann.

'McCann,' asked Ricori, 'do you know a woman named Hortense Darnley?'

'Sure,' answered McCann. 'A blonde doll – she's "Butch" Martin's gal. He took her from the Vanities.'

'Did Peters know her?' I asked.

'Yeah,' said McCann, 'sure he did. She knew Mollie – you know, boss – Peters' kid sister. Mollie quit the Follies about three years ago and he met Hortie at Mollie's. Hortie an' him were both daffy over Mollie's kid. He told me so. But Tom was never gay with her, if that's what you mean.'

I looked sharply at Ricori, remembering distinctly that he had told me Peters had no living relatives. He did not seem in the least disconcerted.

'Where's Martin now, McCann?' he asked.

'Up in Canada, the last I heard of him,' answered McCann. 'Want me to find out?'

'I'll let you know later,' said Ricori, and McCann went back to the hall.

'Is Martin one of your friends or foes?' I asked.

'Neither,' he answered.

I sat silent for a few moments, revolving McCann's surprising information in my mind. The connection that I had vaguely looked for in my assumed proximity of Peters and the woman's dwelling places had been shattered. But McCann had put in its place a stronger link. Hortense Darnley had died October 12 – Peters on November 10. When had Peters last seen the woman? If the mysterious malady were caused by some unknown organism, no one, of course, could tell what its

31

period of incubation might be. Had Peters been infected by her?

'Ricori,' I said, 'twice to-night I have learned that you misled me as to Peters. I'm going to forget it, because I don't believe you'll do it again. And I'm going to trust you, even to the extent of breaking professional confidence. Read these letters.'

I passed him the answers to my questionnaire. He went over them in silence. When he had finished I recounted all that Dr. Y—— had told me of the Darnley case. I told him in detail of the autopsies, including the tiny globes of radiance in the blood of Peters.

At that his face grew white. He crossed himself.

'*La strega!*' he muttered. 'The Witch! The Witchfire!'

'Nonsense, man!' I said. 'Forget your damned superstitions! I want help.'

'You are scientifically ignorant! There are some things, Dr. Lowell—' he began, hotly; then controlled himself.

'What is it you want me to do?'

'First,' I said, 'let's go over these eight cases, analyze them. Braile, have you come to any conclusions?'

'Yes,' Braile answered. 'I think all eight were murdered!'

CHAPTER THREE

The Death and Nurse Walters

That Braile had voiced the thought lurking behind my own mind – and without a shred of evidence so far as I could see to support it – irritated me.

'You're a better man than I am, Sherlock Holmes,' I said sarcastically. He flushed, but repeated stubbornly:

'They were murdered.'

'*La strega!*' whispered Ricori. I glared at him.

'Quit beating around the bush, Braile. What's your evidence.'

'You were away from Peters almost two hours; I was with him practically from start to finish. As I studied him, I had the feeling that the whole trouble was in the mind – that it was not his body, his nerves, his brain, that refused to function, but his will. Not quite that, either. Put it that his will had ceased to care about the functions of the body – and was centered upon killing it!'

'What you're outlining now is not murder but suicide. Well, it has been done. I've watched a few die because they had lost the will to live—'

'I don't mean that,' he interrupted. 'That's passive. This was active—'

'Good God, Braile!' I was honestly shocked. 'Don't tell me you're suggesting all eight passed from the picture by willing themselves out of it – and one of them only an eleven-year-old child!'

'I didn't say that,' he replied. 'What I felt was that

it was not primarily Peters' own will doing it, but another's will, which had gripped his, had wound itself around, threaded itself through, his will. Another's will which he could not, or did not want to resist – at least toward the end.'

'*La maledetta strega!*' muttered Ricori again.

I curbed my irritation and sat considering; after all, I had a wholesome respect for Braile. He was too good a man, too sound, for one to ride roughshod over any idea he might voice.

'Have you any idea as to how these murders, if murders they are, were carried out?' I asked politely.

'Not the slightest,' said Braile.

'Let's consider the murder theory. Ricori, you have had more experience in this line than we, so listen carefully and forget your witch,' I said, brutally enough. 'There are three essential factors to any murder – method, opportunity, motive. Take them in order. First – the method.

'There are three ways a person can be killed by poison or by infection: through the nose – and this includes by gases – through the mouth and through the skin. There are two or three other avenues. Hamlet's father, for example, was poisoned, we read, through the ears, although I've always had my doubts about that. I think, pursuing the hypothesis of murder, we can bar out all approaches except mouth, nose, skin – and, by the last, entrance to the blood can be accomplished by absorption as well as by penetration. Was there any evidence whatever – on the skin, in the membranes of the respiratory channels, in the throat, in the vicera, stomach, blood, nerves, brain – of anything of the sort?'

'You know there wasn't,' he answered.

'Quite so. Then except for the problematical lighted

34

corpuscle, there is absolutely no evidence of method. Therefore we have absolutely nothing in essential number one upon which to base a theory of murder. Let's take number two – opportunity.

'We have a tarnished lady, a racketeer, a respectable spinster, a bricklayer, an eleven-year-old schoolgirl, a banker, an acrobat and a trapeze performer. There, I submit, is about as incongruous a congregation as is possible. So far as we can tell, none of them except conceivably the circus men – and Peters and the Darnley woman – had anything in common. How could anyone, who had opportunity to come in close enough contact to Peters the racketeer to kill him, have equal opportunity to come in similar close contact with Ruth Bailey, the Social Registerite maiden-lady? How could one who had found a way to make contact with banker Marshall come equally close to acrobat Standish? And so on – you perceive the difficulty? To administer whatever it was that caused the deaths – if they were murder – could have been no casual matter. It implies a certain degree of intimacy. You agree?'

'Partly,' he conceded.

'Had all lived in the same neighborhood, we might assume that they might normally have come within range of the hypothetical killer. But they did not—'

'Pardon me, Dr. Lowell,' Ricori interrupted, 'but suppose they had some common interest which brought them within that range.'

'What possible common interest could so divergent a group have had?'

'One common interest is very plainly indicated in these reports and in what McCann has told us.'

'What do you mean, Ricori?'

'Babies,' he answered. 'Or at least – children.'

Braile nodded: 'I noticed that.'

'Consider the reports,' Ricori went on. 'Miss Bailey is described as charitable and devoted to children. Her charities, presumably, took the form of helping them. Marshall, the banker, was interested in child-welfare. The bricklayer, the acrobat and the trapeze performer had children. Anita was a child. Peters and the Darnley woman were, to use McCann's expression, "daffy" over a baby.'

'But,' I objected, 'if they are murders, they are the work of one hand. It is beyond range of possibility that all of the eight were interested in one baby, one child, or one group of children.'

'Very true,' said Braile. 'But all could have been interested in one especial, peculiar thing which they believed would be of benefit to or would delight the child or children to whom each was devoted. And that peculiar article might be obtainable in only one place. If we could find that this is the fact, then certainly that place would bear investigation.'

'It is,' I said, 'undeniably worth looking into. Yet it seems to me that the common-interest idea works two ways. The homes of those who died might have had something of common interest to an individual. The murder, for example, might be a radio adjuster. Or a plumber. Or a collector. An electrician, and so and so on.'

Braile shrugged a shoulder. Ricori did not answer; he sat deep in thought, as though he had not heard me.

'Please listen, Ricori,' I said. 'We've gotten this far. Method of murder – if it is murder – unknown. Opportunity for killing – find some person whose business, profession or what not was a matter of interest to each of the eight, and whom they visited or who visited them;

36

said business being concerned, possibly, in some way with babies or older children. Now for motive. Revenge, gain, love, hate, jealousy, self-protection? – None of these seems to fit, for again we come to the barrier of dissimilar stations in life.'

'How about the satisfaction of an appetite for death – wouldn't you call that a motive?' asked Braile, oddly. Ricori half rose from his chair, stared at him with a curious intentness; then sank back, but I noticed he was now all alert.

'I was about to discuss the possibility of a homicidal maniac,' I said, somewhat testily.

'That's not exactly what I mean. You remember Longfellow's lines:

'I shot an arrow into the air,
    It fell to earth I know not where.'

I've never acquiesced in the idea that was an inspired bit of verse meaning the sending of an argosy to some unknown port and getting it back with a surprise cargo of ivory and peacocks, apes and precious stones. There are some people who can't stand at a window high above a busy street, or on top of a skyscraper, without wanting to throw something down. They get a thrill in wondering who or what will be hit. The feeling of power. It's a bit like being God and unloosing the pestilence upon the just and the unjust alike. Longfellow must have been one of those people. In his heart, he wanted to shoot a real arrow and then mull over in his imagination whether it had dropped in somebody's eye, hit a heart, or just missed someone and skewered a stray dog. Carry this on a little further. Give one of these people power and opportunity to loose death at random, death whose cause he is sure cannot be detected. He sits in his obscurity, in safety, a god of death. With

37

no special malice against anyone, perhaps – impersonal, just shooting his arrows in the air, like Longfellow's archer, for the fun of it.'

'And you wouldn't call such a person a homicidal maniac?' I asked, dryly.

'Not necessarily. Merely free of inhibitions against killing. He might have no consciousness of wrong-doing whatever. Everybody comes into this world under sentence of death – time and method of execution unknown. Well, this killer might consider himself as natural as death itself. No one who believes that things on earth are run by an all-wise, all-powerful God thinks of Him as a homicidal maniac. Yet He looses wars, pestilences, misery, disease, floods, earthquakes – on believers and unbelievers alike. If you believe things are in the hands of what is vaguely termed Fate – would you call Fate a homicidal maniac?'

'Your hypothetical archer,' I said, 'looses a singularly unpleasant arrow, Braile. Also, the discussion is growing far too metaphysical for a simple scientist like me. Ricori, I can't lay this matter before the police. They would listen politely and laugh heartily after I had gone. If I told all that is in my mind to the medical authorities, they would deplore the decadence of a hitherto honored intellect. And I would rather not call in any private detective agency to pursue inquiries.'

'What do you want me to do?' he asked.

'You have unusual resources,' I answered. 'I want you to sift every movement of Peters and Hortense Darnley for the past two months. I want you to do all that is possible in the same way with the others—'

I hesitated.

'I want you to find that one place to which, because of their love for children, each of these unfortunates

38

was drawn. For though my reason tells me you and Braile have not the slightest real evidence upon which to base your suspicions, I grudgingly admit to you that I have a feeling you may be right.'

'You progress, Dr. Lowell,' Ricori said, formally. 'I predict that it will not be long before you will as grudgingly admit the possibility of my witch.'

'I am sufficiently abased,' I replied, 'by my present credulity not to deny even that.'

Ricori laughed, and busied himself copying the essential information from the reports. Ten o'clock struck. McCann came up to say that the car was waiting and we accompanied Ricori to the door. The gunman had stepped out and was on the steps when a thought came to me.

'Where do you begin, Ricori?'

'With Peters' sister.'

'Does she know Peters is dead? '

'No,' he answered, reluctantly. 'She thinks him away. He is often away for long, and for reasons which she understands he is not able to communicate with her directly. At such times I keep her informed. And the reason I have not told her of Peters' death is because she dearly loved him and would be in much sorrow – and – in a month, perhaps, there is to be another baby.'

'Does she know the Darnley woman is dead, I wonder?'

'I do not know. Probably. Although McCann evidently does not.'

'Well,' I said, 'I don't see how you're going to keep Peters' death from her now. But that's your business.'

'Exactly,' he answered, and followed McCann to the car.

Braile and I had hardly gotten back to my library

when the telephone rang. Braile answered it. I heard him curse, and saw that the hand that held the transmitter was shaking. He said: 'We will come at once.'

He set the transmitter down slowly, then turned to me with twitching face.

'Nurse Walters has it!'

I felt a distinct shock. As I have written, Walters was a perfect nurse, and besides that a thoroughly good and attractive young person. A pure Gaelic type – blue black hair, blue eyes with astonishingly long lashes, milk-white skin – yes, singularly attractive. After a moment or two of silence I said:

'Well, Braile, there goes all your fine-spun reasoning. Also your murder theory. From the Darnley woman to Peters to Walters. No doubt now that we're dealing with some infectious disease.'

'Isn't there?' he asked, grimly. 'I'm not prepared to admit it. I happen to know Walters spend most of her money on a little invalid niece who lives with her – a child of eight. Ricori's thread of common interest moves into her case.'

'Nevertheless,' I said as grimly, 'I intend to see that every precaution is taken against an infectious malady.'

By the time we had put on our hats and coats, my car was waiting. The hospital was only two blocks away, but I did not wish to waste a moment. I ordered Nurse Walters removed to an isolated ward used for observation of suspicious diseases. Examining her, I found the same flaccidity as I had noted in the case of Peters. But I observed that, unlike him, her eyes and face showed little of terror. Horror there was, and a great loathing. Nothing of panic. She gave me the same impression of seeing both within and without. As I studied her I distinctly saw a flash of recognition come into her eyes, and with it appeal. I looked at Braile – he nodded; he, too, had seen it.

I went over her body inch by inch. It was unmarked except for a pinkish patch upon her right instep. Closer examination made me think this had been some superficial injury, such as a chafing, or a light burn or scald. If so, it had completely healed; the skin was healthy.

In all other ways her case paralleled that of Peters – and the others. She had collapsed, the nurse told me, without warning while getting dressed to go home. My inquiry was interrupted by an exclamation from Braile. I turned to the bed and saw that Walters' hand was slowly lifting, trembling as though its raising was by some terrific strain of will. The index finger was half-pointing. I followed its direction to the disclosed patch upon the foot. And then I saw her eyes, by that same tremendous effort, focus there.

The strain was too great; the hand dropped, the eyes again were pools of horror. Yet clearly she had tried to convey to us some message, something that had to do with that healed wound.

I questioned the nurse as to whether Walters had said anything to anyone about any injury to her foot. She replied that she had said nothing to her, nor had any of the other nurses spoken of it. Nurse Robbins, however, shared the apartment with Harriet and Diana. I asked who Diana was, and she told me that was the name of Walters' little niece. This was Robbins' night off, I found, and gave instructions to have her get in touch with me the moment she returned to the apartment.

By now Hoskins was taking his samples for the blood tests. I asked him to concentrate upon the microscopic smears and to notify me immediately if he discovered

41

one of the luminous corpuscles. Bartano, an outstanding expert upon tropical diseases, happened to be in the hospital, as well as Somers, a brain specialist in whom I had strong confidence. I called them in for observation, saying nothing of the previous cases. While they were examining Walters, Hoskins called up to say he had isolated one of the shining corpuscles. I asked the pair to go to Hoskins and give me their opinion upon what he had to show them. In a little while they returned, somewhat annoyed and mystified. Hoskins, they said, had spoken of a 'leucocyte containing a phosphorescent nucleus.' They had looked at the slide but had been unable to find it. Somers very seriously advised me to insist upon Hoskins having his eyes examined. Bartano said caustically that he would have been quite as surprised to have seen such a thing as he would have been to have observed a miniature mermaid swimming around in an artery. By these remarks, I realized afresh the wisdom in my silence.

Nor did the expected changes in expression occur. The horror and loathing persisted, and were commented upon by both Bartano and Somers as 'unusual'. They agreed that the condition must be caused by a brain lesion of some kind. They did not think there was any evidence either of microbic infection or of drugs or poison. Agreeing that it was a most interesting case, and asking me to let them know its progress and outcome, they departed.

At the beginning of the fourth hour, there was a change of expression, but not what I had been expecting. In Walters' eyes, on her face, was only loathing. Once I thought I saw a flicker of the devilish anticipation flash over her face. If so, it was quickly mastered. About the middle of the fourth hour, we saw recognition again return to her eyes. Also, there was a perceptible rally of the slowing heart. I sensed an intense gathering of nervous force.

And then her eyelids began to rise and fall, slowly, as though by tremendous effort, in measured time and – purposefully. Four times they raised and lowered; there was a pause; then nine times they lifted and fell; again the pause, then they closed and opened once. Twice she did this—

'She's trying to signal,' whispered Braile. 'But what?'

Again the long-lashed lids dropped and rose – four times . . . pause . . . nine times . . . pause . . . once . . .

'She's going,' whispered Braile.

I knelt, stethoscope at ears . . . slower . . . slower . . . beat the heart . . . and slower . . . and stopped.

'She's gone!' I said, and arose. We bent over her, waiting for that last hideous spasm, convulsion – whatever it might be.

It did not come. Stamped upon her dead face was the loathing, and that only. Nothing of the devilish glee. Nor was there sound from her dead lips. Beneath my hand I felt the flesh of her white arm begin to stiffen.

The unknown death had destroyed Nurse Walters – there was no doubt of that. Yet in some obscure, vague way I felt that it had not conquered her.

Her body, yes. But not her will!

CHAPTER FOUR

The Thing in Ricori's Car

I returned home with Braile, profoundly depressed. It is difficult to describe the effect the sequence of events I am relating had upon my mind from beginning to end – and beyond the end. It was as though I walked almost constantly under the shadow of an alien world, nerves prickling as if under surveillance of invisible things not of our life . . . the subconsciousness forcing itself to the threshold of the conscious battering at the door between and calling out to be on guard . . . every moment to be on guard. Strange phrases for an orthodox man of medicine? Let them stand.

Braile was pitiably shaken. So much so that I wondered whether there had been more than professional interest between him and the dead girl. If there had been, he did not confide in me.

It was close to four o'clock when we reached my house. I insisted that he remain with me. I called the hospital before retiring, but they had heard nothing of Nurse Robbins. I slept a few hours, very badly.

Shortly after nine, Robbins called me on the telephone. She was half hysterical with grief. I bade her come to my office, and when she had done so Braile and I questioned her.

'About three weeks ago,' she said, 'Harriet brought home to Diana a very pretty doll. The child was enraptured. I asked Harriet where she had gotten it, and she said in a queer little store way down town.

' "Job," she said – my name is Jobina— "There's the

44

queerest woman down there. I'm sort of afraid of her, Job."

'I didn't pay much attention. Besides, Harriet wasn't ever very communicative. I had the idea she was a bit sorry she had said what she had.

'Now I think of it though, Harriet acted rather funny after that. She'd be gay and then she'd be – well, sort of thoughtful. About ten days ago she came home with a bandage around her foot. The right foot? Yes. She said she'd been having tea with the woman she'd gotten Diana's doll from. The teapot upset and the hot tea had poured down on her foot. The woman had put some salve on it right away, and now it didn't hurt a bit.

' "But I think I'll put something on it I know something about," she told me. Then she slipped off her stocking and began to strip the bandage. I'd gone into the kitchen and she called to me to come and look at her foot.

' "It's queer," she said. "That was a bad scald, Job. Yet it's practically healed. And that salve hasn't been on more than an hour."

'I looked at her foot. There was a big red patch on the instep. But is wasn't sore, and I told her the tea couldn't have been very hot.

' "But it was really scalded, Job," she said. "I mean it was blistered."

'She sat looking at the bandage and at her foot for quite a while. The salve was bluish and had a queer shine to it. I never saw anything like it before. No, I couldn't detect any odor to it. Harriet reached down and took the bandage and said:

' "Job, throw it in the fire."

'I threw the bandage in the fire. I remember that it gave a queer sort of flicker. It didn't seem to burn. It

45

just flickered and then it wasn't there. Harriet watched it, and turned sort of white .Then she looked at her foot again.

' "Job," she said. "I never saw anything heal as quick as that. She *must* be a witch!'

' "What on earth are you talking about, Harriet?" I asked her.

' "Oh, nothing," she said. "Only I wish I had the courage to rip that place on my foot wide open – and rub in an antidote for snake-bite!"

'Then she laughed, and I thought she was fooling. But she painted it with iodine and bandaged it with an antiseptic besides. The next morning she woke me up and said:

' "Look at that foot now. Yesterday a whole pot of scalding tea poured over it. And now it isn't even tender. And the skin ought to be just smeared off. Job, I wish to the Lord it was!'

'That's all, Dr. Lowell. She didn't say any more about it and neither did I. And she just seemed to forget all about it. Yes. I did ask her where the shop was and who the woman was, but she wouldn't tell me. I don't know why.

'And after that I never knew her so gay and care-free. Happy, careless . . . Oh, I don't know why she should have died . . . I don't . . . I don't!'

Braile asked:

'Do the numbers 491 mean anything to you, Robbins? Do you associate them with any address Harriet knew?'

She thought, then shook her head. I told her of the measured closing and opening of Walters' eyes.

'She was clearly attempting to convey some message in which those numbers figured. Think again.'

46

Suddenly she straightened, and began counting upon her fingers. She nodded.

'Could she have been trying to spell out something? If they were letters they would read d, i and a. They're the first three letters of Diana's name.'

Well, of course that seemed the simple explanation. She might have been trying to ask us to take care of the child. I suggested this to Braile. He shook his head.

'She knew I'd do that,' he said. 'No, it was something else.'

A little after Robbins had gone, Ricori called up. I told him of Walters' death. He was greatly moved. And after that came the melancholy business of the autopsy. The results were precisely the same as in that of Peters'. There was nothing whatever to show why the girl had died.

At about four o'clock the next day Ricori again called me on the telephone.

'Will you be at home between six and nine, Dr. Lowell?' There was suppressed eagerness in his voice.

'Certainly, if it is important,' I answered, after consulting my appointment book. 'Have you found out anything, Ricori?'

He hesitated.

'I do not know. I think perhaps – yes.'

'You mean,' I did not even try to hide my own eagerness. 'You mean – the hypothetical place we discussed?'

'Perhaps. I will know later. I go now to where it may be.'

'Tell me this, Ricori – what do you expect to find?'

'Dolls!' he answered.

And as though to avoid further questions he hung up before I could speak.

Dolls!

I sat thinking. Walters had bought a doll. And in that same unknown place where she had bought it, she had sustained the injury which had so worried her – or rather, whose unorthodox behavior had so worried her. Nor was there doubt in my mind, after hearing Robbins' story, that it was to that injury she had attributed her seizure, and had tried to tell us so. We had not been mistaken in our interpretation of that first desperate effort of will I have described. She might, of course, have been in error. The scald or, rather, the salve had had nothing whatever to do with her condition. Yet Walters had been strongly interested in a child. Children were the common interest of all who had died as she had. And certainly the one great common interest of children is dolls. What was it that Ricori had discovered?

I called Braile, but could not get him. I called up Robbins and told her to bring the doll to me immediately, which she did.

The doll was a peculiarly beautiful thing. It had been cut from wood, then covered with gesso. It was curiously life-like. A baby doll, with an elfin little face. Its dress was exquisitely embroidered, a folk-dress of some country I could not place. It was, I thought, almost a museum piece, and one whose price Nurse Walters could hardly have afforded. It bore no mark by which either maker or seller could be identified. After I had examined it minutely, I laid it away in a drawer. I waited impatiently to hear from Ricori.

At seven o'clock there was a sustained, peremptory ringing of the doorbell. Opening my study door, I heard McCann's voice in the hall, and called to him to come up. At first glance I knew something was very wrong. His tight-mouthed tanned face was a sallow yellow, his eyes held a dazed look. He spoke from stiff lips:

'Come down to the car. I think the boss is dead.'

'Dead!' I exclaimed, and was down the stairs and out beside the car in a breath. The chauffeur was standing beside the door. He opened it, and I saw Ricori huddled in a corner of the rear seat. I could feel no pulse, and when I raised the lids of his eyes they stared at me sightlessly. Yet he was not cold.

'Bring him in,' I ordered.

McCann and the chauffeur carried him into the house and placed him on the examination table in my office. I bared his breast and applied the stethoscope. I could detect no sign of the heart functioning. Nor was there, apparently, any respiration. I made a few other rapid tests. To all appearances, Ricori was quite dead. And yet – I was not satisfied. I did the things customary in doubtful cases, but without results.

McCann and the chauffeur had been standing close beside me. They read my verdict in my face. I saw a strange glance pass between them; and obviously each of them had a touch of panic, the chauffeur more markedly than McCann. The latter asked in a level, monotonous voice:

'Could it have been poison?'

'Yes, it could—' I stopped.

Poison! And that mysterious errand about which he had telephoned me! And the possibility of poison in the other cases! But this death – and again I felt the doubt – had not been like those others.

'McCann,' I said, 'when and where did you first notice anything wrong?'

He answered, still in that monotonous voice:

49

'About six blocks down the street. The boss was sitting close to me. All at once he says "Jesu!" Like he's scared. He shoves his hands up to his chest. He gives a kind of groan an' stiffens out. I says to him: 'What's the matter, boss, you got a pain?' He don't answer me, an' then he sort of falls against me an' I see his eyes is wide open. He looks dead to me. So I yelps to Paul to stop the car and we both look him over. Then we beat it here like hell.'

I went to a cabinet and poured them stiff drinks of brandy. They needed it. I threw a sheet over Ricori.

'Sit down,' I said, 'and you, McCann, tell me exactly what occurred from the time you started out with Mr. Ricori to wherever it was he went. Don't skip a single detail.'

He said:

'About two o'clock the boss goes to Mollie's – that's Peters' sister – stays an hour, comes out, goes home and tells Paul to be back at four-thirty. But he's doing a lot of 'phoning so we don't start till five. He tells Paul where he wants to go, a place over in a little street down off Battery Park. He says to Paul not to go through the street, just park the car over by the Battery. And he says to me, "McCann, I'm going in this place myself. I don't want 'em to know I ain't by myself." He says, "I got reasons. You hang around an' look in now an' then, but don't come in unless I call you." I say, "Boss, do you think it's wise?" An' he says, "I know what I'm doing an' you do what I tell you." So there ain't any argument to that.

'We get down to this place an' Paul does like he's told, an' the boss walks up the street an' he stops at a little joint that's got a lot of dolls in the window. I looks in the place as I go past. There ain't much light but I see a lot of other dolls inside an' a thin gal at a counter. She looks white as a fish's belly to me, an' after the boss has stood at the window a minute or two he goes in, an' I go by slow to look at the gal again because she sure looks whiter than I ever saw a gal look who's on her two feet. The boss is talkin' to the gal who's showing him some dolls. The next time I go by there's a woman in the place. She's so big, I stand at the window a minute to look at her because I never see anybody that looks like her. She's got a brown face an' it looks sort of like a horse, an' a little mustache an' moles, an' she's as funny a looking brand as the fish-white gal. Big an' fat. But I get a peep at her eyes – Geeze, what eyes! Big an' black an' bright, an' somehow I don't like them any more than the rest of her. The next time I go by, the boss is over in a corner with the big dame. He's got a wad of bills in his hand and I see the gal watching sort of frightened like. The next time I do my beat, I don't see either the boss or the woman.

'So I stand looking through the window because I don't like the boss out of my sight in this joint. An' the next thing I see is the boss coming out of a door at the back of the shop. He's madder than hell an' carrying something an' the woman is behind him an' her eyes spitting fire. The boss is jabbering but I can't hear what he's saying, an' the dame is jabbering too an' making funny passes at him. Funny passes? Why, funny motions with her hands. But the boss heads for the door an' when he gets to it I see him stick what he's carrying inside his overcoat an' button it up round it.

'It's a doll. I see its legs dangling down before he gets it under his coat. A big one, too, for it makes quite a bulge—'

He paused, began mechanically to roll a cigarette,

51

then glanced at the covered body and threw the cigarette away. He went on:

'I never see the boss so mad before. He's muttering to himself in Italian an' saying something over an' over that sounds like "strayga." I see it ain't no time to talk so I just walk along with him. Once he says to me, more as if he's talking to himself than me, if you get what I mean – he says, "The Bible says you shall not suffer a witch to live." Then he goes on muttering an' holding one arm fast over this doll inside his coat.

'We get to the car an' he tells Paul to beat it straight to you an' to hell with traffic – that's right, ain't it, Paul? Yes. When we get in the car he stops muttering an' just sits there quiet, not saying anything to me until I hear him say "Jesu!" like I told you. And that's all, ain't it, Paul?'

The chauffeur did not answer. He sat staring at McCann with something of entreaty in his gaze. I distinctly saw McCann shake his head. The chauffeur said, in a strongly marked Italian accent, hesitatingly:

'I do not see the shop, but everything else McCann say is truth.'

I got up and walked over to Ricori's body. I was about to lift the sheet when something caught my eye. A red spot about as big as a dime – a blood stain. Holding it in place with one finger, I carefully lifted the edge of the sheet. The blood spot was directly over Ricori's heart.

I took one of my strongest glasses and one of my finest probes. Under the glass, I could see on Ricori's breast a minute puncture, no larger than that made by a hypodermic nedle. Carefully I inserted the probe. It slipped easily in and in until it touched the wall of the heart. I went no further.

Some needle-pointed, exceedingly fine instrument had been thrust through Ricori's breast straight into his heart!

I looked at him, doubtfully; there was no reason why such a minute puncture should cause death. Unless, of course, the weapon which had made it had been poisoned or there had been some other violent shock which had contributed to that of the wound itself. But such shock or shocks might very well bring about in a person of Ricori's peculiar temperament some curious mental condition, producing an almost perfect counterfeit of death. I had heard of such cases.

No, despite my tests, I was not sure Ricori was dead. But I did not tell McCann that. Alive or dead, there was one sinister fact that McCann must explain. I turned to the pair, who had been watching me closely.

'You say there were only the three of you in the car?'

Again I saw a glance pass between them.

'There was the doll,' McCann answered, half-defiantly. I brushed the answer aside, impatiently.

'I repeat: there were only the three of you in the car?'

'Three – men, yes.'

'Then,' I said grimly, 'you two have a lot to explain. Ricori was stabbed. I'll have to call the police.'

McCann arose and walked over to the body. He picked up the glass and peered through it at the tiny puncture. He looked at the chauffeur. He said:

'I told you the doll done it, Paul!'

CHAPTER FIVE

The Thing in Ricori's Car
CONTINUATION

I said, incredulously, 'McCann, you surely don't expect *me* to believe that?'

He did not answer, rolling another cigarette which this time he did not throw away. The chauffeur staggered over to Ricori's body; he threw himself on his knees and began mingled prayers and implorations. McCann, curiously enough, was now completely himself. It was as though the removal of uncertainty as to the cause of Ricori's death had restored all his old cold confidence. He lighted the cigarette; he said, almost cheerfully:

'I'm aiming to make you believe.'

I walked over to the telephone. McCann jumped in front of me and stood with his back against the instrument.

'Wait a minute, Doc. If I'm the kind of a rat that'll stick a knife in the heart of the man who hired me to protect him – ain't it occurred to you the spot you're on ain't so healthy? What's to keep me an' Paul from giving you the works an' making our getaway?'

Frankly, that had not occurred to me. Now I realized in what a truly dangerous position I was placed. I looked at the chauffeur. He had risen from his knees and was standing, regarding McCann intently.

'I see you get it.' McCann smiled, mirthlessly. He walked to the Italian. 'Pass your rods, Paul.'

Without a word the chauffeur dipped into his pockets and handed him a pair of automatics. McCann laid them on my table. He reached under his left arm and placed another pistol beside them; reached into his pocket and added a second.

'Sit there, Doc,' he said, and indicated my chair at the table. 'That's all our artillery. Keep the guns right under your hands. If we make any breaks, shoot. All I ask is you don't do any calling up till you've listened.'

I sat down, drawing the automatics to me, examining them to see that they were loaded. They were.

'Doc,' McCann said, 'there's three things I want you to consider. First, if I'd had anything to do with smearing the boss, would I be giving you a break like this? Second, I was sitting at his right side. He had on a thick overcoat. How could I reach over an' run anything as thin as whatever killed him must have been all through his coat, an' through the doll, an' through his clothes, an' through him without him putting up some kind of a fight. Hell, Ricori was a strong man. Paul would have seen us—'

'What difference would that have made,' I interrupted, 'if Paul were an accomplice?'

'Right,' he acquiesced, 'that's so. Paul's as deep in the mud as I am. Ain't that so, Paul?' He looked sharply at the chauffeur, who nodded. "All right, we'll leave that with a question mark after it. Take the third point – if I'd killed the boss that way, an' Paul was in it with me, would we have took him to the one man who'd be expected to know how he was killed? An' then when you'd found out as expected, hand you an alibi like this? Christ, Doc, I ain't loco enough for that!'

His face twitched.

'Why would I want to kill him? I'd a-gone through hell an' back for him an' he knew it. So would've Paul.'

I felt the force of all this. Deep within me I was conscious of a stubborn conviction that McCann was telling the truth – or at least the truth as he saw it. He had not stabbed Ricori. Yet to attribute the act to a doll was too fantastic. And there had been only the three men in the car. McCann had been reading my thoughts with an uncanny precision.

'It might've been one of them mechanical dolls,' he said. 'Geared up to stick.'

'McCann, go down and bring it up to me,' I said sharply – he had voiced a rational explanation.

'It ain't there,' he said, and grinned at me again mirthlessly. 'It jumped out!'

'Preposterous—' I began. The chauffeur broke in:

'It's true. Something jump out. When I ope' the door. I think it cat, dog, maybe. I say, 'What the hell—' Then I see it. It run like hell. It stoop. It duck in shadow. I see it just as flash an' then no more. I say to McCann— "What the hell!" McCann, he's feeling around bottom of car. He say— "It's the doll. It done for the boss!" I say: "Doll! What you mean doll?" He tell me. I know nothing of any doll before. I see the boss carry something in his coat, *si*. But I don't know what. But I see one goddam thing that don't look like cat, dog. It jump out of car, through my legs, *si*!'

I said ironically: 'Is it your idea, McCann, that this mechanical doll was geared to run away as well as to stab?'

He flushed, but answered quietly:

'I ain't saying it was a mechanical doll. But anything else would be – well, pretty crazy, wouldn't it?'

'McCann,' I asked abruptly, 'what do you want me to do?'

'Doc, when I was down Arizona way, there was a ranchero died. Died sudden. There was a feller looked as if he had a lot to do with it. The marshal said: "Hombre, I don't think you done it – but I'm the lone one on the jury. What say?" The hombre say, "Marshal, give me two weeks, an' if I don't bring in the feller that done it, you hang me." The marshal says, "Fair enough. The temporary verdict is deceased died by shock." It was shock all right. Bullet shock. All right, before the two weeks was up, along comes this feller with the murderer hog-tied to his saddle.'

'I get your point, McCann. But this isn't Arizona.'

'I know it ain't. But couldn't you certify it was heart disease? Temporarily? An' give me a week? Then if I don't come through, shoot the works. I won't run away. It's this way, Doc. If you tell the bulls, you might just as well pick up one of them guns an' shoot me an' Paul dead right now. If we tell the bulls about the doll, they'll laugh themselves sick an' fry us at Sing Sing. If we don't, we fry anyway. If by a miracle the bulls drop us – there's them in the boss's crowd that'll soon remedy that. I'm telling you, Doc, you'll be killing two innocent men. An' worse, you'll never find out who did kill the boss, because they'll never look any further than us. Why should they?'

A cloud of suspicion gathered around my conviction of the pair's innocence. The proposal, naïve as it seemed, was subtle. If I assented, the gunman and the chauffeur would have a whole week to get away, if that was the plan. If McCann did not come back, and I told the truth of the matter, I would be an accessory after the fact – in effect, co-murderer. If I pretended that my

57

suspicions had only just been aroused, I stood, at the best, convicted of ignorance. If they were captured, and recited the agreement, again I could be charged as an accessory. It occurred to me that McCann's surrender of the pistols was extraordinarily clever. I could not say that my assent had been constrained by threats. Also, it might have been only a cunningly conceived gesture to enlist my confidence, weaken my resistance to his appeal. How did I know that the pair did not have still other weapons, ready to use if I refused?

Striving to find a way out of the trap, I walked over to Ricori. I took the precaution of dropping the automatics into my pockets as I went. I bent over Ricori. His flesh was cold, but not with the peculiar chill of death. I examined him once more, minutely. And now I could detect the faintest of pulsation in the heart . . . a bubble began to form at the corner of his lips . . . Ricori lived!

I continued to bend over him, thinking faster than ever I had before. Ricori lived, yes. But it did not lift my peril. Rather it increased it. For if McCann had stabbed him, if the pair had been in collusion, and learned that they had been unsuccessful, would they not finish what they had thought ended? With Ricori alive, Ricori able to speak and to accuse them – a death more certain than the processes of law confronted them. Death at Ricori's command at the hands of his henchmen. And in finishing Ricori they would at the same time be compelled to kill me.

Still bending, I slipped a hand into my pocket, clenched an automatic, and then whirled upon them with the gun leveled.

'Hands up! Both of you!' I said.

Amazement flashed over McCann's face, consternation over the chauffeur's. But their hands went up.

I said, 'There's no need of that clever little agreement, McCann. Ricori is not dead. When he's able to talk he'll tell what happened to him.'

I was not prepared for the effect of this announcement. If McCann was not sincere, he was an extraordinary actor. His lanky body stiffened. I had seldom seen such glad relief as was stamped upon his face. Tears rolled down his tanned cheeks. The chauffeur dropped to his knees, sobbing and praying. My suspicions were swept away. I did not believe this could be acting. In some measure I was ashamed of myself.

'You can drop your hands, McCann,' I said, and slipped the automatic back in my pocket.

He said, hoarsely: 'Will he live?'

I answered: 'I think he has every chance. If there's no infection, I'm sure of it.'

'Thank God!' whispered McCann, and over and over, 'Thank God!'

And just then Braile entered, and stood staring in amazement at us.

'Ricori has been stabbed. I'll explain the whole matter later,' I told him. 'Small puncture over the heart and probably penetrating it. He's suffering mainly from shock. He's coming out of it. Get him up to the Annex and take care of him until I come.'

Briefly I reviewed what I had done and suggested the immediate further treatment. And when Ricori had been removed, I turned to the gunmen.

'McCann,' I said, 'I'm not going to explain. Not now. But here are your pistols, and Paul's. I'm giving you your chance.'

He took the automatics looking at me with a curious gleam in his eyes.

'I ain't saying I wouldn't like to know what touched you off, Doc,' he said. 'But whatever you do is all right by me – if only you can bring the boss around.'

'Undoubtedly there are some who will have to be notified of his condition,' I replied. 'I'll leave that all to you. All I know is that he was on his way to me. He had a heart attack in the car. You brought him to me. I am now treating him – for heart attack. If he should die, McCann – well, that will be another matter.'

'I'll do the notifying,' he answered. 'There's only a couple that you'll have to see. Then I'm going down to that doll joint an' get the truth outa that hag.'

His eyes were slits, his mouth a slit, too.

'No,' I said, firmly. 'Not yet. Put a watch on the place. If the woman goes out, discover where she goes. Watch the girl as closely. If it appears as though either of them are moving away – running off – let them. But follow them. I don't want them molested or even alarmed until Ricori can tell what happened there.'

'All right,' he said, but reluctantly.

'Your doll story,' I reminded him, sardonically, 'would not be so convincing to the police as to my somewhat credulous mind. Take no chance of them being injected into the matter. As long as Ricori is alive, there is no need of them being so injected.'

I took him aside.

'Can you trust the chauffeur to do no talking?'

'Paul's all right,' he said.

'Well, for both your sakes, he would better be.' I warned.

They took their departure. I went up to Ricori's room. His heart was stronger, his respiration weak but encouraging. His temperature, although still dangerously subnormal, had improved. If, as I had told Mc-

Cann, there was no infection, and if there had been no poison nor drug upon the weapon with which he had been stabbed, Ricori should live.

Later that night two thoroughly polite gentlemen called upon me, heard my explanation of Ricori's condition, asked if they might see him, did see him, and departed. They assured me that 'win or lose' I need have no fear about my fees, nor have any hesitancy in bringing in the most expensive consultants. In exchange, I assured them that I believed Ricori had an excellent chance to recover. They asked me to allow no one to see him except themselves, and McCann. They thought it might save me trouble to have a couple of men whom they would send to me, to sit at the door of the room – outside, of course, in the hall. I answered that I would be delighted.

In an exceedingly short time two quietly watchful men were on guard at Ricori's door, just as they had been over Peters'.

In my dreams that night dolls danced around me, pursued me, threatened me. My sleep was not pleasant.

CHAPTER SIX

Strange Experience of Officer Shevlin

Morning brought a marked improvement in Ricori's condition. The deep coma was unchanged, but his temperature was nearly normal; respiration and heart action quite satisfactory. Braile and I divided duties so that one of us could be constantly within call of the nurses. The guards were relieved after breakfast by two others. One of my quiet visitors of the night before made his appearance, looked at Ricori and received with unfeigned gratification my reassuring reports.

After I had gone to bed the obvious idea had occurred to me that Ricori might have made some memorandum concerning his quest; I had felt reluctance about going through his pockets, however. Now seemed to be the opportunity to ascertain whether he had or had not. I suggested to my visitor that he might wish to examine any papers Ricori had been carrying, adding that we had been interested together in a certain matter, that he had been on his way to discuss this with me when he had undergone his seizure; and that he might have carried some notes of interest to me. My visitor agreed; I sent for Ricori's overcoat and suit and we went through them. There were a few papers, but nothing relating to our investigation.

In the breast pocket of his overcoat, however, was a curious object – a piece of thin cord about eight inches long in which had been tied nine knots, spaced at irregular intervals. They were curious knots too, not quite like any I could recollect having observed. I studied the cord with an unaccountable but distinct feeling of uneasiness. I glanced at my visitor and saw a puzzled look in his eyes. And then I remembered Ricori's superstition, and reflected that the knotted cord was probably a talisman or charm of some sort. I put it back in the pocket.

When again alone, I took it out and examined it more minutely. The cord was of human hair, tightly braided – the hair a peculiarly pale ash and unquestionably a woman's. Each knot, I now saw, was tied differently. Their structure was complex. The difference between them, and their irregular spacing, gave a vague impression of forming a word or sentence. And, studying the knots, I had the same sensation of standing before a blank door, vitally important for me to open, that I had felt while watching Peters die. Obeying some obscure impulse, I did not return the cord to the pocket but threw it into the drawer with the doll which Nurse Robbins had brought me.

Shortly after three, McCann telephoned me. I was more than glad to hear from him. In the broad light of day his story of the occurrence in Ricori's car had become incredibly fantastic, all my doubts returning. I had even begun again to review my unenviable position if he disappeared. Some of this must have shown in the cordiality of my greeting, for he laughed.

'Thought I'd rode off the range, did you, Doc? You couldn't drive me away. Wait till you see what I got.'

I awaited his arrival with impatience. When he appeared he had with him a sturdy, red-faced man who carried a large paper clothing-bag. I recognized him as a policeman I had encountered now and then on the Drive, although I had never before seen him out of uniform. I bade the two be seated, and the officer sat on the edge of a chair, holding the clothes-bag gingerly across his knees. I looked at McCann, inquiringly.

'Shevlin,' he waved his hand at the officer, 'said he knew you, Doc. But I'd have brought him along, anyway.'

'If I didn't know Dr. Lowell, it's not me that'd be here McCann me lad,' said Shevlin, glumly. 'But it's brains the Doc has got in his head, an' not a cold boiled potato like that damned lootenant.'

'Well,' said McCann, maliciously, 'the Doc'll prescribe for you anyway, Tim.'

' 'Tis no prescribin' I want, I tell you,' Shevlin bellowed, 'I seen it wit' me own eyes, I'm tellin' you. An' if Dr. Lowell tells me I was drunk or crazy I'll tell him t'hell wit' him, like I told the lootenant. An' I'm tellin' you, too, McCann.'

I listened to this with growing amazement.

'Now, Tim, now, Tim,' soothed McCann, 'I believe you. You don't know how much I want to believe you – or why, either.'

He gave me a quick glance, and I gathered that whatever the reason he had brought the policeman to see me, he had not spoken to him of Ricori.

'You see, Doc, when I told you about that doll getting up an' jumping out of the car you thought I was loco. All right, I says to me, maybe it didn't get far. Maybe it was one of them improved mechanical dolls, but even if it was it has to run down sometime. So I goes hunting for somebody else that might have seen it. An' this morning I runs into Shevlin here. An' he tells me. Go on, Tim, give the Doc what you gave me.'

Shevlin blinked, shifted the bag cautiously and began. He had the dogged air of repeating a story that he had told over and over. And to unsympathetic audiences; for as he went on he would look at me defiantly, or raise his voice belligerently.

'It was one o'clock this mornin'. I am on me beat when I hear somebody yellin' desperate like. "Help!" he yells. "Murder! Take it away!" he yells. I go runnin', an' there standin' on a bench is a guy in his soup-an'-nuts an' high hat jammed over his ears, an' a-hittin' this way an' that wit' his cane, an' a-dancin' up an' down an' it's him that's doin' the yellin'.

'I reach over an' tap him on the shins wit' me night-club, an' he looks down an' then flops right in me arms. I get a whiff of his breath an' I think I see what's the matter wit' him all right. I get him on his feet, an' I says: "Come on now, the pink'll soon run off the ele-phants," I says. "It's this Prohibition hooch that makes it look so thick," I says. "Tell me where you live an' I'll put you in a taxi, or do you want t'go to a hospital?" I says.

'He stands there a-holdin' unto me an' a-shakin', an' he says: "D'ye think I'm drunk?" An' I begins t'tell him. "An' how—," when I looks at him, an' he ain't drunk. He might've *been* drunk, but he ain't drunk now. An' all t'once he flops down on the bench an' pulls up his socks, an' I sees blood runnin' from a dozen little holes, an' he says, "Maybe you'll be tellin' me it's pink ele-phants done that?"

'I looks at 'em an' feels 'em, an' it's blood all right, as if somebody's been jabbin' a hat-pin in him—'

Involuntarily I stared at McCann. He did not meet my eyes. Imperturbably he was rolling a cigarette—

'An' I says: "What the hell done it?" An' he says – "The doll done it!"'

A little shiver ran down my back, and I looked again

at the gunman. This time he gave me a warning glance. Shevlin glared up at me.

' "The doll done it!" he tells me,' Shevlin shouted. 'He tells me the doll done it!'

McCann chuckled and Shevlin turned his glare from me to him. I said hastily:

'I understand, Officer. He told you it was the doll made the wounds. An astonishing assertion, certainly.'

'Y'don't believe it, y'mean?' demanded Shevlin, furiously.

'I believe he told you that, yes,' I answered. 'But go on.'

'All right, would y'be sayin' I was drunk too, t'believe it? Fer it's what that potato-brained lootenant did.'

'No, no,' I assured him hastily. Shevlin settled back, and went on:

'I asks the drunk, "What's her name?" "What's whose name?" says he. "The doll's," I says. "I'll bet you she was a blonde doll," I says, "an' wants her picture in the tabloids. The brunettes don't use hatpins," I says. "They're all fer the knife."

' "Officer," he says, solemn, "it was a doll. A little man doll. An' when I say doll I mean a doll. I was walkin' along," he says, "gettin' the air. I won't deny I'd had some drinks," he says, "but nothin' I couldn't carry. I'm swishin' along wit' me cane, when I drops it by that bush there," he says, pointin'. "I reach down to pick it up," he says, "an' there I see a doll. It's a big doll an' it's all huddled up crouchin'. as if somebody dropped it that way. I reaches over t' pick it up. As I touch it, the doll jumps as if I hit a spring. It jumps right over me head," he says. "I'm surprised," he says, "an' considerably startled, an' I'm crouchin' there lookin' where the doll was when I feel a hell of a pain in the calf of me leg," he says, "like I been stabbed. I jump up, an' there's this doll wit' a big pin in its hand just ready t' jab me again."

' "Maybe," says I to the drunk, "maybe 'twas a midget you seen?" "Midget hell!" says he, "it was a doll! an' it was jabbin' me wit' a hat-pin. It was about two feet high," he says, "wit' blue eyes. It was grinnin' at me in a way that made me blood run cold. An' while I stood there paralyzed, it jabbed me again. I jumped on the bench," he says, "an' it danced around an' around, an' it jumped up an' jabbed me. An' it jumped down an' up again an' jabbed me. I thought it meant to kill me, an' I yelled like hell," says the drunk. "An' who wouldn't?" he asks me. "An' then you come," he says, "an' the doll ducked into the bushes there. Fer God's sake, officer, come wit' me till I can get a taxi an' go home," he says, "fer I make no bones tellin' you I'm scared right down to me gizzard!" says he.

'So I take the drunk by the arm,' went on Shevlin, thinkin', poor lad, what this bootleg booze'll make you see, but still puzzled about how he got them holes in his legs. We come out to the Drive. The drunk is still a-shakin' an' I'm a-waitin' to hail a taxi, when all of a sudden he lets out a squeal – "There it goes! Look, there it goes!"

'I follow his finger, an' sure enough I see somethin' scuttlin' over the sidewalk an' out on the Drive. The light's none too good, an' I think it's a cat or maybe a dog. Then I see there's a little coupé drawn up opposite at the curb. The cat or dog, whatever it is, seems to be makin' fer it. The drunk's still yellin' an' I'm tryin' to see what it is, when down the Drive hell-fer-leather comes a big car. It hits this thing kersmack an' never stops. He's out of sight before I can raise me whistle. I think I see the thing wriggle an' I think, still thinkin' it's a cat or dog, "I'll put you out of your misery," an' I run over to it wit' me gun. As I do so the coupé that's been waitin' shoots off hell-fur-leather too. I get over to what the other car hit, an' I look at it—'

He slipped the bag off his knees, set it down beside him and untied the top.

'An' this is what it was.'

Out of the bag he drew a doll, or what remained of it, The automobile had gone across its middle, crushing it. One leg was missing; the other hung by a thread. Its clothing was torn and begrimed with the dirt of the roadway. It was a doll – but uncannily did it give the impression of a mutilated pygmy. Its neck hung limply over its breast.

McCann stepped over and lifted the doll's head—

I stared, and stared . . . with a prickling of the scalp . . . with a slowing of the heart beat . . .

For the face that looked up at me, blue eyes glaring, was the face of Peters!

And on it, like the thinnest of veils, was the shadow of that demonic exultance I had watched spread over the face of Peters after death had stilled the pulse of his heart!

CHAPTER SEVEN

The Peters Doll

Shevlin watched me as I stared at the doll. He was satisfied by its effect upon me.

'A hell of a lookin' thing, ain't it?' he asked. 'The doctor sees it, McCann. I told you he had brains!' He jounced the doll down upon his knee, and sat there like a red-faced ventriloquist with a peculiarly malevolent dummy – certainly it would not have surprised me to have heard the diabolic laughter issue from its faintly grinning mouth.

'Now, I'll tell you, Dr. Lowell,' Shevlin went on. 'I stands there lookin' at this doll, an' I picks it up. "There's more in this than meets the eye, Tim Shevlin," I says to myself. An' I look to see what's become of the drunk. He's standin' where I left him, an' I walk over to him an' he says: "Was it a doll like I told you? Hah! I told you it was a doll! Hah! That's him!" he says, gettin' a peek at what I'm carryin'. So I say to him, "Young fellow, me lad, there's somethin' wrong here. You're goin' to the station wit' me an' tell the lootenant what you told me an' show him your legs an' all," I says. An' the drunk says, "Fair enough, but keep that thing on the other side of me." So we go to the station.

'The lootenant's there an' the sergeant an' a coupla flatties. I marches up an' sticks the doll on the top of the desk in front of the lootenant.

' "What's this?" he says, grinnin'. "Another kidnapin'?"

69

' "Show him your legs," I tells the drunk. "Not unless they're better than the Follies," grins this potato-brained ape. But the drunk's rolled up his pants an' down his socks an' shows 'em.

' "What t'hell done that?" says the lootenant, standin' up.

' "The doll," says the drunk. The lootenant looks at him, and sits back blinkin'. An' I tells him about answerin' the drunk's yells, an' what he tells me, an' what I see. The sergeant laughs an' the flatties laugh but the lootenant gets red in the face an' says, "Are you tryin' to kid me, Shevlin?" An' I says, "I'm tellin' you what he tells me an' what I seen, an' there's the doll." An' he says, "This bootleg is fierce but I never knew it was catchin'." An' he crooks his finger at me an' says, "Come up here, I want t' smell your breath." An' then I knows it's all up, because t' tell the truth the drunk had a flask an' I'd took one wit' him. Only one an' the only one I'd had. But there it was on me breath. An' the lootenant says, "I thought so. Get down."

'An' then he starts bellerin' an' hollerin' at the drunk —"You wit' your soup-an'-nuts an' your silk hat, you ought to be a credit to your city an' what t' hell you thing you can do, corrupt a good officer an' kid me? You done the first but you ain't doin' the second," he yelps. "Put him in the cooler," he yelps. "An' throw his damned doll in wit' him t' keep him company!" 'An' at that the drunk lets out a screech an' drops t' the floor. He's out good an' plenty. An' the lootenant says, "The poor damned fool . . . by God he believes his own lie! Bring him around an' let him go." An' he says t' me, "If you weren't such a good man, Tim, I'd have you up for this. Take your degen'ret doll an' go home," he says, "I'll send a relief t' your beat. An' take t-morrow off an' sober up," says he. An' I says t'him, "All right, but I seen what I seen. An' t' hell wit' you all!" I says t' the flatties. An' everybody's laughin' fit t' split. An' I says t' the lootenant. "If you break me for it or not, t' hell wit' you too." But they keep on laughin', so I take the doll an' walk out.'

He paused.

'I take the doll home,' he resumed. 'I tell it all t' Maggie, me wife. An' what does she tell me?' "T' think you've been off the hard stuff or near off so long," she says, "an' now look at you!" she says, "wit' this talk of stabbin' dolls, an' insultin' the lootenant, an' maybe gettin' sent t' Staten Island," she says. "An' Jenny just gettin' in high school! Go t' bed," she says, "an' sleep it off, an' throw the doll in the garbage," she says. But by now I am gettin' good an' mad, an' I do not throw it in the garbage but I take it wit' me. An' awhile ago I meet McCann, an' somehow he knows somethin.' I tell him an' he brings me here. An' just fer what, I don't know.'

'Do you want me to speak to the lieutenant?' I asked.

'What could you say?' he replied, reasonably enough. 'If you tell him the drunk was right, an' that I'm right an' I did see the doll run, what'll he think? He'll think you're as crazy as I must be. An' if you explain maybe I was a little off me nut just for the minute, it's to the hospital they'll be sendin' me. No, Doctor. I'm much obliged, but all I can do is say nothin' more an' be dignified an' maybe hand out a shiner or two if they get too rough. It's grateful I am fer the kindly way you've listened. It makes me feel better.'

Shevlin got to his feet, sighing heavily.

'An' what do you think? I mean about what the

drunk said he seen, an' what I seen?' he asked somewhat nervously.

'I cannot speak for the inebriate,' I answered cautiously. 'As for yourself – well, it might be that the doll had been lying out there in the street, and that a cat or dog ran across just as the automobile went by. Dog or cat escaped, but the action directed your attention to the doll and you thought—'

He interrupted me with a wave of his hand.

'All right. All right. 'Tis enough. I'll just leave the doll wit' you to pay for the diagnoses, sir.'

With considerable dignity and perceptibly heightened color Shevlin stalked from the room. McCann was shaking with silent laughter. I picked up the doll and laid it on my table. I looked at the subtly malignant little face – and I did not feel much like laughing.

For some obscure reason I took the Walters doll out of the drawer and placed it beside the other, took out the strangely knotted cord and set it between them. McCann was standing at my side, watching. I heard him give a low whistle.

'Where did you get that, Doc?' he pointed to the cord. I told him. He whistled again.

'The boss never knew he had it, that's sure,' he said. 'Wonder who slipped it over on him? The hag, of course. But how?'

'What are you talking about?' I asked.

'Why, the witch's ladder,' he pointed again to the cord. 'That's what they call it down Mexico way. It's bad medicine. The witch slips it to you and then she has power over you . . .' He bent over the cord . . . 'Yep, it's the witch's ladder – the nine knots an' woman's hair . . . an' in the boss's pocket!'

72

He stood staring at the cord. I noticed he made no attempt to pick it up.

'Take it up and look at it closer, McCann,' I said.

'Not me!' He stepped back. 'I'm telling you it's bad medicine, Doc.'

I had been steadily growing more and more irritated against the fog of superstition gathering ever heavier around me, and now I lost my patience.

'See here, McCann,' I said, hotly, 'are you, to use Shevlin's expression, trying to kid me? Every time I see you I am brought face to face with some fresh outrage against credibility. First it is your doll in the car. Then Shevlin. And now your witch's ladder. What's your idea?'

He looked at me with narrowed eyes, a faint flush reddening the high cheek-bones.

'The only idea I got,' he drawled more slowly than usual, 'is to see the boss on his feet. An' to get whoever got him. As for Shevlin – you don't think he was faking, do you?'

'I do not,' I answered. 'But I am reminded that you were beside Ricori in the car when he was stabbed. And I cannot help wondering how it was that you discovered Shevlin so quickly to-day.'

'Meaning by that?' he asked.

'Meaning,' I answered, 'that your drunken man has disappeared. Meaning that it would be entirely possible for him to have been your confederate. Meaning that the episode which so impressed the worthy Shevlin could very well have been merely a clever bit of acting, and the doll in the street and the opportunely speeding automobile a carefully planned maneuver to bring about the exact result it had accomplished. After all, I have only your word and the chauffeur's word that the

73

doll was not down in the car the whole time you were here last night. Meaning that—'

I stopped, realizing that, essentially, I was only venting upon him the bad temper aroused by my perplexity.

'I'll finish for you,' he said. 'Meaning that I'm the one behind the whole thing.'

His face was white, and his muscles tense.

'It's a good thing for you that I like you, Doc,' he continued. 'It's a better thing for you that I know you're on the level with the boss. Best of all, maybe that you're the only one who can help him – if he can be helped. That's all.'

'McCann,' I said, 'I'm sorry, deeply sorry. Not for what I said, but for having to say it. After all, the doubt is there. And it is a reasonable doubt. You must admit that. Better to spread it before you than keep it hidden.'

'What might be my motive?'

'Ricori has powerful enemies. He also has powerful friends. How convenient to his enemies if he could be wiped out without suspicion, and a physician of highest repute and unquestionable integrity be inveigled into giving the death a clean bill of health. It is my professional pride, not personal egotism, that I am that kind of a physician, McCann.'

He nodded. His face softened and I saw the dangerous tenseness relax .

'I've no argument, Doc. Not on that or nothing else you've said. But I'm thanking you for your high opinion of my brains. It'd certainly take a pretty clever man to work all this out this-a-way. Sort of like one of them cartoons that shows seventy-five gimcracks set to drop a brick on a man's head at exactly twenty minutes, sixteen seconds after two in the afternoon. Yeah, I must be clever!'

I winced at this broad sarcasm, but did not answer. McCann took up the Peters doll and began to examine it. I went to the 'phone to ask Ricori's condition. I was halted by an exclamation from the gunman. He beckoned me, and handing me the doll, pointed to the collar of its coat. I felt about it. My fingers touched what seemed to be the round head of a large pin. I pulled out as though from a dagger sheath a slender piece of metal nine inches long. It was thinner than an average hat-pin, rigid and needle-pointed.

Instantly I knew that I was looking upon the instrument that had pierced Ricori's heart!

'Another outrage!' McCann drawled. 'Maybe I put it there, Doc!'

'You could have, McCann.'

He laughed. I studied the queer blade – for blade it surely was. It appeared to be of finest steel, although I was not sure it was that metal. Its rigidity was like none I knew. The little knob at the head was half an inch in diameter and less like a pinhead than the haft of a poniard. Under the magnifying glass it showed small grooves upon it . . . as though to make sure the grip of a hand . . . a doll's hand . . . a doll's dagger! There were stains upon it.

I shook my head impatiently, and put the thing aside, determining to test those stains later. They were bloodstains, I knew that, but I must make sure. And yet, if they were, it would not be certain proof of the incredible – that a doll's hand had used this deadly thing.

I picked up the Peters doll and began to study it minutely. I could not determine of what it was made. It was not of wood, like the other doll. More than anything else, the material resembled a fusion of gum and wax. I knew of no such composition. I stripped it of the clothing. The undamaged part of the doll was anatomically perfect. The hair was human hair, carefully planted in the scalp. The eyes were blue crystals of some kind. The clothing showed the same extraordinary skill in the making as the clothes of Diana's doll.

I saw now that the dangling leg was not held by a thread. It was held by a wire. Evidently the doll had been molded upon a wire frame-work. I walked over to my instrument cabinet, and selected a surgical saw and knives.

'Wait a minute, Doc.' McCann had been following my movements. 'You going to cut this thing apart?'

I nodded. He reached into his pocket, pulled out a heavy hunting knife. Before I could stop him, he had brought its blade down like an ax across the neck of the Peters doll. It cut through it cleanly. He took the head and twisted it. A wire snapped. He dropped the head on the table, and tossed the body to me. The head rolled. It came to rest against the cord he had called the witch's ladder.

The head seemed to twist and to look up at us. I thought for an instant the eyes flared redly, the features to contort, the malignancy intensify – as I had seen it intensify upon Peters' living face . . . I caught myself up, angrily . . . a trick of the light, of course . . . I turned to McCann and swore.

'Why did you do that?'

'You're worth more to the boss than I am,' he said, cryptically.

I did not answer. I cut open the decapitated body of the doll. As I had suspected, it had been built upon a wire frame-work. As I cut away the encasing material, I found this frame-work was a single wire, or a single metal strand, and that as cunningly as the doll's body

76

had been shaped, just as cunningly had this wire been twisted into an outline of the human skeleton!

Not, of course, with minute fidelity, but still with amazing accuracy ... there were no joints nor articulations ... the substance of which the doll was made was astonishingly pliant ... the little hands flexible ... it was more like dissecting some living mannikin than a doll. ... And it was rather – dreadful. ...

I glanced toward the severed head. ...

McCann was bending over it, staring down into its eyes, his own not more than a few inches away from the glinting blue crystals. His hands clutched the table edge and I saw that they were strained and tense as though he were making a violent effort to push himself away. When he had tossed the head upon the table it had come to rest against the knotted cord – but now that cord was twisted around the doll's severed neck and around its forehead as though it were a small serpent!

And distinctly I saw that McCann's face was moving closer ... slowly closer ... to that tiny one ... as though it were being drawn to it ... and that in the little face a living evil was concentrated ... and that McCann's face was a mask of horror ...

'McCann!' I cried, and thrust an arm under his chin, jerking back his head. And as I did this I could have sworn the doll's eyes turned to me, and that its lips writhed.

'McCann staggered back. He stared at me for a moment, and then leaped to the table. He picked up the doll's head, dashed it to the floor and brought his heel down upon it again and again, like one stamping out the life of a venomous spider. Before he ceased, the head was a shapeless blotch, all semblance of humanity or anything else crushed out of it – but within it the two blue crystals that had been its eyes still glinted, and the knotted cord of the witch's ladder still wound through it.

'God! It was . . . was drawing me down to it . . .'

McCann lighted a cigarette with shaking hand, tossed the match away. The match fell upon what had been the doll's head.

There followed, simultaneously, a brilliant flash, a disconcerting sobbing sound and a wave of intense heat. Where the crushed head had been there was now only an irregularly charred spot upon the polished wood. Within it lay the blue crystals that had been the eyes of the doll – lusterless and blackened. The knotted cord had vanished.

And the body of the doll had disappeared. Upon the table was a nauseous puddle of black waxy liquid out of which lifted the ribs of the wire skeleton!

The Annex phone rang; mechanically I answered it.

'Yes,' I said. 'What is it?'

'Mr. Ricori, sir. He's out of the coma. He's awake!'

I turned to McCann.

'Ricori's come through!'

He gripped my shoulders – then drew a step away, a touch of awe on his face.

'Yeah?' whispered McCann. 'Yeah – he came through when the knots burned! It freed him! It's you an' me that's got to watch our step now!'

CHAPTER EIGHT

Nurse Walters' Diary

I took McCann up with me to Ricori's bedside. Confrontation with his chief would be the supreme test, I felt, resolving one way or another all my doubts as to his sincerity. For I realized, almost immediately, that bizarre as had been the occurrences I have just narrated, each and all of them could have been a part of the elaborate hocus-pocus with which I had tentatively charged the gunman. The cutting off of the doll's head could have been a dramatic gesture designed to impress my imagination. It was he who had called my attention to the sinister reputation of the knotted cord. It was McCann who had found the pin. His fascination by the severed head might have been assumed. And the tossing of the match a calculated action designed to destroy evidence. I did not feel that I could trust my own peculiar reactions as valid.

And yet – it was difficult to credit McCann with being so consummate an actor, so subtle a plotter. Ah, but he could be following the instructions of another mind capable of such subtleties. I wanted to trust McCann. I hoped that he would pass the test. Very earnestly I hoped it.

The test was ordained to failure. Ricori was fully conscious, wide awake, his mind probably as alert and sane as ever. But the lines of communication were still down. His mind had been freed, but not his body. The paralysis persisted, forbidding any muscular movements except the deep-seated unconscious reflexes. His eyes looked up at me, bright and intelligent, but from an expressionless face . . . looked up at McCann with the same unchanging stare. . . .

McCann whispered. 'Can he hear?'

'I thing so, but he has no way of telling us.'

The gunman knelt beside the bed and took Ricori's hands in his. He said, clearly: 'Everything's all right, boss. We're all on the job.'

Not the utterance nor the behavior of a guilty man – but then I had told him Ricori could not answer. I said to Ricori:

'You're coming through splendidly. You've had a severe shock, and I know the cause. I'd rather you were this way for a day or so than able to move about. I have a perfectly good medical reason for this. Don't worry, don't fret, try not to think of anything unpleasant. Let your mind relax. I'm going to give you a mild hypo. Don't fight it. Let yourself sleep.'

I gave him the hypodermic, and watched with satisfaction its quick effect. It convinced me that he had heard.

I returned to my study with McCann. I was doing some hard thinking. There was no knowing how long Ricori would remain in the grip of the paralysis. He might awaken in a hour fully restored, or it might hold him for days. In the meantime there were three things I felt it necessary to ascertain. The first that a thorough watch was being kept upon the place where Ricori had gotten the doll; second, that everything possible be found out about the two women McCann had described; third, what it was that had made Ricori go there. I had determined to take the gunman's value – for the moment at least. At the same time, I did not want to

80

admit him into my confidence any more than was necessary.

'McCann,' I began, 'have you arranged to keep the doll store under constant surveillance, as we agreed last night?'

'You bet. A flea couldn't hop in or out without being spotted.'

'Any reports?'

'The boys ringed the joint close to midnight. The front's all dark. There's a building in the back an' a space between it an' the rear of the joint. There's a window with a heavy shutter, but a line of light shows under it. About two o'clock this fish-white gal comes slipping up the street and lets in. The boys at the back hear a hell of a squalling, an' then the light goes out. This morning the gal opens the shop. After a while the hag shows up, too. They're covered, all right.'

'What have you found out about them?'

'The hag calls herself Madame Mandilip. The gal's her niece. Or so she says. They rode in about eight months since. Nobody knows where from. Pay their bills regular. Seem to have plenty of money. Niece does all the marketing. The old woman never goes out. Keep to themselves like a pair of clams. Have strictly nothing to do with the neighbors. The hag has a bunch of special customers – rich-looking people many of them. Does two kinds of trade, it looks – regular dolls an' what goes with 'em, an' special dolls which they say the old woman's a wonder at. Neighbors ain't a bit fond of 'em. Some of 'em think she's handling dope. That's all – yet.'

Special dolls? Rich people?

Rich people like the spinster Bailey, the banker Marshall?

Regular dolls – for people like the acrobat, the bricklayer? But these might have been 'special' too, in ways McCann could not know.

'There's the store,' he continued. 'Back of it two or three rooms. Upstairs a big room like a storeroom. They rent the whole place. The hag an' the wench, they live in the rooms behind the store.'

'Good work!' I applauded, and hesitated— 'McCann, did the doll remind you of somebody?'

He studied me with narrowed eyes.

'*You* tell *me*,' he said at last, dryly.

'Well – I thought it resembled Peters.'

'*Thought* it resembled!' he exploded. '*Resembled* – hell! It was the lick-an'-spit of Peters!'

'Yet you said nothing to me of that. Why?' I asked, suspiciously.

'Well I'm damned—' he began, then caught himself. 'I knowed you seen it. I thought you kept quiet account of Shevlin, an' followed your lead. Afterwards you were so busy putting me through the jumps there wasn't a chance.'

'Whoever made that doll must have known Peters quite well.' I passed over this dig. 'Peters must have sat for the doll as one sits for an artist or a sculptor. Why did he do it? When did he do it? Why did anyone desire to make a doll like him?'

'Let me work on the hag for an hour an' I'll tell you,' he answered, grimly.

'No,' I shook my head. 'Nothing of that sort until Ricori can talk. But maybe we can get some light in another way. Ricori had a purpose in going to that store. I know what it was. But I do not know what directed his attention to the store. I have reason to believe it was information he gained from Peters' sister. Do you know her well enough to visit her and to draw from her what it was she told Ricori yesterday? Casually – tactfully – without telling her of Ricori's illness?'

He said, bluntly: 'Not without you give me more of a lead – Mollie's no fool.'

'Very well. I am not aware whether Ricori told you, but the Darnley woman is dead. We think there is a connection between her death and Peters' death. We think that it has something to do with the love of both of them for Mollie's baby. The Darnley woman died precisely as Peters did—'

He whispered – 'You mean with the same – trimmings?'

'Yes. We had reason to think that both might have picked up the – the disease – in the same place. Ricori thought that perhaps Mollie might know something which would identify that place. A place where both of them might have gone, not necessarily at the same time, and have been exposed to – the infection. Maybe even a deliberate infection by some ill-disposed person. Quite evidently what Ricori learned from Mollie sent him to the Mandilips. There is one awkward thing, however – unless Ricori told her yesterday, she does not know her brother is dead.'

'That's right,' he nodded. 'He gave orders about that.'

'If he did not tell her, you must not.'

'You're holding back quite a lot, ain't you, Doc?' He drew himself up to go.

'Yes,' I said, frankly. 'But I've told you enough.'

'Yeah? Well, maybe.' He regarded me, somberly. 'Anyway, I'll soon know if the boss broke the news to Mollie. If he did, it opens up the talk natural. If he didn't – well, I'll call you up after I've talked to her. *Hasta luego.*'

83

With this half-mocking adieu he took his departure. I went over to the remains of the doll upon the table. The nauseous puddle had hardened. In hardening it had roughly assumed the aspect of a flattened human body. It had a peculiarly unpleasant appearance, with the miniature ribs and the snapped wire of the spine glinting above it. I was overcoming my reluctance to collect the mess for analysis when Braile came in. I was so full of Ricori's awakening, and of what had occurred, that it was some time before I noticed his pallor and gravity. I stopped short in the recital of my doubts regarding McCann to ask him what was the matter.

'I woke up this morning thinking of Harriet,' he said. 'I knew the 4-9-1 code, if it was a code, could not have meant Diana. Suddenly it struck me that it might mean Diary. The idea kept haunting me. When I had a chance I took Robbins and went to the apartment. We searched, and found Harriet's diary. Here it is.'

He handed me a little red-bound book. He said: 'I've gone through it.'

I opened the book. I set down the parts of it pertinent to the matter under review.

—NOV. 3. Had a queer sort of experience today. Dropped down to Battery Park to look at the new fishes in the Aquarium. Had an hour or so afterwards and went poking around some of the old streets, looking for something to take home to Diana. Found the oddest little shop. Quaint and old looking with some of the loveliest dolls and dolls' clothes in the window I've ever seen. I stood looking at them and peeping into the shop through the window. There was a girl in the shop. Her back was turned to me. She turned suddenly and looked at me. She gave me the queerest kind of shock. Her face was white, without any color whatever and her eyes were wide and sort of staring and frightened. She had a lot of hair, all ashen blonde and piled up on her head. She was the strangest looking girl I think I've ever seen. She stared at me for a full minute and I at her. Then she shook her head violently and made motions with her hands for me to go away. I was so astonished I could hardly believe my eyes. I was about to go in and ask her what on earth was the matter with her when I looked at my watch and found I had just time to get back to the hospital. I looked into the shop again and saw a door at the back beginning slowly to open. The girl made one last and it seemed almost *despairing* gesture. There was something about it that suddenly made me want to run. But I didn't. I did walk away though. I've puzzled about the thing all day. Also, besides being curious I'm a bit angry. The dolls and clothes are beautiful. What's wrong with me as a customer? I'm going to find out.

—NOV. 5. I went back to the doll shop this afternoon. The mystery deepens. Only I don't think it's much of a mystery. I think the poor thing is a bity crazy. I didn't stop to look in the window but went right in the door. The white girl was at a little counter at the back. When she saw me her eyes looked more frightened than ever and I could see her tremble. I went up to her and she whispered – 'Oh, why did you come back? I told you to go away!' I laughed, I couldn't help it, and I said: 'You're the queerest shopkeeper I ever met. Don't you want people to buy your things?' She said low and very quickly: 'It's too late! You can't go now! But don't touch anything. Don't touch anything she gives you. Don't touch anything she points out to you.' And then

85

in the most everyday way she said quite clearly: 'Is there anything I can show you? We have everything for dolls.' The transition was so abrupt that it was startling. Then I saw that a door had opened in the back of the shop, the same door I had seen opening before, and that a woman was standing in it looking at me.

I gaped at her I don't know how long. She was so truly extraordinary. She must be almost six feet and heavy, with enormous breasts. Not fat. Powerful. She has a long face and her skin is brown. She has a distinct mustache and a mop of iron-gray hair. It was her eyes that held me spellbound. They are simply enormous! Black and so full of life! She must have a tremendous vitality. Or maybe it is the contrast with the white girl who seems to be drained of life. No, I'm sure she has a most unusual vitality. I had the queerest thrill when she was looking at me. I thought, nonsensically – 'What big eyes you have, grandma!' 'The better to see you with, my dear!' 'What big teeth you have, grandma!' 'The better to eat you with, my dear!' (*I'm not so sure though that it was all nonsense.*) And she really has big teeth, strong and yellow. I said, quite stupidly: 'How do you do?' She smiled and touched me with her hand and I felt another queer thrill. Her hands are the most beautiful I ever saw. So beautiful, they are uncanny. Long with tapering fingers and so white. Like the hands El Greco or Botticelli put on their women. I suppose that is what gave me the odd shock. They don't seem to belong to her immense coarse body at all. But neither do the eyes. The hands and the eyes go together. Yes, that's it.

She smiled and said: 'You love beautiful things.' Her voice belongs to hands and eyes. A deep rich glowing contralto. I could feel it go through me like an organ chord. I nodded. She said: 'Then you shall see them, my dear. Come.' She paid no attention to the girl. She turned to the door and I followed her. As I went through the door I looked back at the girl. She appeared more frightened than ever and distinctly I saw her lips form the word – 'Remember.'

The room she led me into was – well, I can't describe it. It was like her eyes and hands and voice. When I went into it I had the strange feeling that I was no longer in New York. Nor in America. Nor *anywhere* on earth, for that matter. I had the feeling that the only *real* place that existed was the room. It was frightening. The room was larger than it seemed possible it could be, judging from the size of the store. Perhaps it was the light that made it seem so. A soft mellow, *dusky* light. It is exquisitely paneled, even the ceiling. On one side there is nothing but these beautiful old dark panelings with carvings in very low relief covering them. There is a fireplace and a fire was burning in it. It was unusually warm but the warmth was not oppressive. There was a faint fragrant odor, probably from the burning wood. The furniture is old and exquisite too, but unfamiliar. There are some tapestries, clearly ancient. It is curious, but I find it difficult to recall clearly just what is in that room. All that is clear is its unfamiliar beauty. I do remember clearly an immense table, and I recall thinking of it as a 'baronial board.' And I remember intensely the round mirror, and I don't like to think of that.

I found myself telling her all about myself and about Diana, and how she loved beautiful things. She listened, and said in that deep, sweet voice, 'She shall have one beautiful thing, my dear.' She went to a cabinet and came to me with the loveliest doll I have ever seen. It made me gasp when I thought how Di would love it. A little baby doll, and so life-like and exquisite. 'Would she like that?' she asked. I said: 'But I could never afford such a treasure. I'm poor.' And she laughed, and said: 'But *I* am not poor. This shall be yours when I have finished dressing it.' It was rude, but I could not help saying: 'You must be very, very rich to have all these lovely things. I wonder why you keep a doll store.' And she laughed again and said, 'Just to meet nice people like you, my dear.'

It was then I had the peculiar experience, with the mirror. It was round and I had looked and looked at it because it was like, I thought, the half of an immense globule of clearest water. Its frame was brown wood elaborately carved, and now and then the reflection of the carvings seemed to dance in the mirror like vegetation on the edge of a woodland pool when a breeze ruffles it. I had been wanting to look into it, and all at once the desire became irresistible. I walked to the mirror. I could see the whole room reflected in it. Just as though I were looking not at its image or my own image but into another similar room with a similar me peering out. And then there was a wavering and the reflection of the room became misty, although the reflection of myself was perfectly clear. Then I could see only myself, and I seemed to be getting smaller and smaller until I was no bigger than a large doll. I brought my face closer and the little faces thrust itself forward. I shook my head and smiled, and it did the same. It was my reflection – but so *small*! And suddenly I felt frightened and shut my eyes tight. And when I looked in the mirror again everything was as it had been before.

I looked at my watch and was appalled at the time

I had spent. I arose to go, still with the panicky feeling at my heart. She said: 'Visit me again tomorrow, my dear. I will have the doll ready for you.' I thanked her and said I would. She went with me to the door of the shop. The girl did not look at me as I passed through.

Her name is Madame Mandilip. I am not going to her to-morrow nor ever again. She fascinates me but she makes me afraid. I don't like the way I felt before the round mirror. And when I first looked into it and saw the whole room reflected, why didn't I see her image in it? I did not! And although the room was lighted, I can't remember seeing any windows or lamps. And that girl! And yet – Di would love the doll so!

—NOV. 7. Queer how difficult it is to keep to my resolution not to return to Madame Mandilip. It makes me so restless! Last night I had a terrifying dream. I thought I was back in that room. I could see it distinctly. And suddenly I realized *I was looking out into it*. And that I was *inside the mirror*. I knew I was little. Like a doll. I was frightened and I beat against it, and fluttered against it like a moth against a windowpane. Then I saw two beautiful long white hands stretching out to me. They opened the mirror and caught me and I struggled and fought and tried to get away. I woke with my heart beating so hard it nigh smothered me. Di says I was crying out: 'No! No! I won't! No, I won't!' over and over. She threw a pillow at me and I suppose that's what awakened me.

To-day I left the hospital at four, intending to go right home. I don't know what I could have been thinking about, but whatever it was I must have been mighty preoccupied. I woke up to find myself in the Subway

Station just getting on a Bowling Green train. That would have taken me to the Battery. I suppose absent-mindedly I had set out for Madame Mandilip's. It gave me such a start that I almost *ran* out of the station and up to the street. I think I'm acting very stupidly. I always have prided myself on my common sense. I think I must consult Dr. Braile and see whether I'm becoming neurotic. There's no earthly reason why I shouldn't go to see Madame Mandilip. She is *most* interesting and certainly showed she liked me. It was so *gracious* of her to offer me that lovely doll. She must think me ungrateful and rude. And it would *please* Di so. When I think of how I've been feeling about the mirror it makes me feel as childish as Alice in Wonderland – or Through the Looking-Glass, rather. Mirrors or any other reflecting surfaces make you see queer things sometimes. Probably the heat and the fragrance had a lot to do with it. I *really* don't know that Madame Mandilip wasn't reflected. I was too intent upon looking at myself. It's too absurd to run away and hide like a child from a witch. Yet that's precisely what I'm doing. If it weren't for that girl – but she *certainly* is a neurotic! I want to go, and I just don't see why I'm behaving so.

—NOV. 10. Well, I'm glad I didn't persist in that ridiculous idea. Madame Mandilip is *wonderful*. Of course, there are some queer things I don't understand, but that's because she is so different from any one I've ever met and because when I get inside her room life becomes so different. When I leave, it's like going out of some enchanted castle into the prosiest kind of world. Yesterday afternoon I determined I'd go to see her straight from the hospital. The moment I made up my mind I felt as though a cloud had lifted from it. Gayer and happier than I've been for a week. When I went in the store the white girl – her name is Laschna – stared at me as though she was going to cry. She said, in the oddest choked voice, 'Remember that I tried to save you!'

It seemed so funny that I laughed and laughed. Then Madame Mandilip opened the door, and when I looked at her eyes and heard her voice I knew why I was so light-hearted – it was like coming home after the most *awful* siege of home-sickness. The lovely room welcomed me. It really did. It's the only way I can describe it. I have the queer feeling that the room is as alive as Madame Mandilip. That it is a part of her – or rather, a part of the part of her that are her eyes and hands and voice. She didn't ask me why I had stayed away. She brought out the doll. It is more wonderful than ever. She has still some work to do on it. We sat and talked, and then she said: 'I'd like to make a doll of you, my dear.' Those were her exact words, and for just an instant I had a frightened feeling because I remembered my dream and saw myself fluttering inside the mirror and trying to get out. And then I realized it was just her way of speaking, and that she meant she would like to make a doll that looked like me. So I laughed and said, 'Of course you can make a doll of me, Madame Mandilip.' I wonder what nationality she is.

She laughed with me, her big eyes bigger than ever and very bright. She brought out some wax and began to model my head. Those beautiful long fingers worked rapidly as though each of them was a little artist in itself. I watched them, fascinated. I began to get sleepy, and sleepier and sleepier. She said, 'My dear, I *do* wish you'd take off your clothes and let me model your whole body. Don't be shocked. I'm just an old woman.' I didn't mind at all, and I said sleepily, 'Why, of course you can.' And I stood on a little stool and watched the wax taking shape under those white fingers until it had become a small and most perfect copy of me. I knew it was perfect, although I was so sleepy I could hardly see it. I was so sleepy Madame Mandilip had to help me dress, and then I must have gone sound asleep, because I woke up with quite a start to find her patting my hands and saying, 'I'm sorry I tired you, child. Stay if you wish. But if you must go, it is growing late.' I looked at my watch and I was still so sleepy I could hardly see it, but I knew it *was* dreadfully late. Then Madame Mandilip pressed her hands over my eyes and suddenly I was wide awake. She said, 'Come to-morrow and take the doll.' I said, 'I must pay you what I can afford.' She said, 'You've paid me in full, my dear, by letting me make a doll of you.' Then we both laughed and I hurried out. The white girl was busy with someone, but I called 'au 'voir' to her. Probably she didn't hear me, for she didn't answer.

—NOV. 11. I have the doll and Diana is crazy about it! How glad I am I didn't surrender to that silly morbid feeling. Di has never had anything that has given her such happiness. She adores it! Sat again for Madame Mandilip this afternoon for the finishing touches on my own doll. She is a genius. *Truly* a genius! I wonder more than ever why she is content to run a little shop. She surely could take her place among the greatest of artists. The doll literally is *me*. She asked if she could cut some of my hair for its head and of course I let her. She tells me this doll is not the real doll she is going to make of me. That will be much larger. This is just the model from which she will work. I told her I thought this was perfect but she said the other would be of less perishable material. Maybe she will give me this one after she is finished with it. I was so anxious to take the baby doll home to Di that I didn't stay long. I smiled and spoke to Laschna as I went out, and she nodded to me although not very cordially. I wonder if she can be jealous.

—NOV. 13. This is the first time I have felt like writing since that dreadful case of Mr. Peters on the morning of the 10th. I had just finished writing about Di's doll when the hospital called to say they wanted me on duty that night. Of course, I said I would come. Oh, but I wish I hadn't. I'll never forget that dreadful death. Never! I don't want to write or think about it. When I came home that morning I could not sleep, and I tossed and tossed trying to get his face out of my mind. I thought I had schooled myself too well to be affected by any patient. But there was something—. Then I thought that if there was anyone who could help me to forget, it would be Madame Mandilip. So about two o'clock I went down to see her. Madame was in the store with Laschna and seemed surprised to see me so early. And not so pleased as usual, or so I thought but perhaps it was my nervousness. The moment I entered the lovely room I began to feel better. Madame had been doing something with wire on the table but I couldn't see what because she made me sit in a big comfortable chair, saying, 'You look tired, child. Sit here and rest until I'm finished and here's an old picture book that will keep you interested.' She gave me a queer old book, long and narrow and it must have been very old because it was on vellum or something and the pictures and their colorings were like some of those books that have come down from the Middle Ages, the kind the old monks used to paint. They were all scenes in forests or gardens and the flowers and trees were the *queerest*! There were no people or anything in them but you had the strangest feeling that if you had just a little better eyes you could see people or something behind them. I mean it was as though they were hiding behind the trees and flowers or among them and looking out at you. I don't know how long I studied the pictures, trying and trying to see those hidden folk, but at last Madame called me. I went to the table with the book still in my hand. She said, 'That's for the doll I am making of you. Take it up and see how cleverly it is done.' And she pointed to something made of wire on the table. I reached out to pick it up and then suddenly I saw that it was a skeleton. It was little, like a child's skeleton and all at once the face of Mr. Peters flashed in my mind and I screamed in a moment of perfectly crazy panic and threw out my hands. The book flew out of my hand and dropped on the little wire skeleton and there was a sharp twang and the skeleton seemed to jump. I recovered myself immediately and I saw that the end of the wire had come loose and had cut the binding of the book and was still stuck in it. For a moment Madame was dreadfully angry. She caught my arm and squeezed it so it hurt and her eyes were furious and she said in the strangest voice, 'Why did you do that? Answer me. Why?' And she actually shook me. I don't blame her now, although then she really did frighten me, because she must have thought I did it deliberately. Then she saw how I was trembling and her eyes and voice became gentle and she said, 'Something is troubling you, my dear. Tell me and perhaps I can help you.'

She made me lie down upon a divan and sat beside me and stroked my hair and forehead and though I never discuss our cases to others I found myself pouring out the whole story of the Peters case. She asked who was the man who had brought him to the hospital and I said Dr. Lowell called him Ricori and I supposed he was the notorious gangster. Her hands made me feel quiet and nice and sleepy and I told her about Dr. Lowell and how great a doctor he is and how terrible I am in love in secret with Dr. B——, I'm sorry I told her about the case. Never have I done such a thing. But I was so shaken and once I had begun I seemed to have to tell her everything. Everything in my mind was so distorted that once when I had lifted my head to look at her I actually thought she was *gloating*. That shows how little I was like myself! After I had finished she told me to lie there and sleep and she would waken me when I wished. So I said I must go at four. I went right to sleep and woke up feeling rested and fine. When I went out the little skeleton and book were still on the table, and I said I was so sorry about the book. She said, 'Better the book than your hand, my dear. The wire might have snapped loose while you were handling it and given you a nasty cut.' She wants me to bring down my nurse's dress so she can make a little one like it for the new doll.

—NOV. 14. I wish I'd never gone to Madame Mandilip's. I wouldn't have had my foot scalded. But that's not the real reason I'm sorry. I couldn't put it in words if I tried. But I do wish I *hadn't*. I took the nurse's costume down to her this afternoon. She made a little model of it very quickly. She was gay and sang me some of the most haunting little songs. I couldn't understand the

95

words. She laughed when I asked her what the language was and said, 'The language of the people who peeped at you from the pictures of the book, my dear.' That was a strange thing to say. How did she know I thought there were people hidden in the pictures? I *do* wish I'd never gone there. She brewed some tea and poured cups for us. And then just as she was handing me mine her elbow struck the teapot and overturned it and the scalding tea poured right down over my right foot. It pained atrociously. She took off the shoe and stripped off the stocking and spread salve of some sort over the scald. She said it would take out the pain and heal it immediately. It did stop the pain, and when I came home I could hardly believe my eyes. Job wouldn't believe it had really been scalded. Madame Mandilip was *terribly* distressed about it. At least she *seemed* to be. I wonder why she didn't go to the door with me as usual. She didn't. She stayed in the room. The white girl, Laschna, was close to the door when I went out into the store. She looked at the bandage on my foot and I told her it had been scalded but Madame had dressed it. She didn't even say she was sorry. As I went out I looked at her and said a bit angrily, 'Good-by.' Her eyes filled with tears and she looked at me in the strangest way and shook her head and said 'Au 'voir!' I looked at her again as I shut the door and the tears were rolling down her cheeks. I wonder why? (*I wish I had never gone to Madame Mandilip!!*)

—NOV. 15. Foot all healed. I haven't the slightest desire to return to Madame Mandilip's. I shall never go there again. I wish I could destroy that doll she gave me for Di. But it would break the child's heart.

—NOV. 20. Still no desire to see her. I find I'm forgetting all about her. The only time I think of her is when I see Di's doll. I'm *glad*! So glad I want to dance and sing. I'll never see her again.

But dear God how I wish I never had seen her! And still I don't know why.

This was the last reference to Madame Mandilip in Nurse Walters' diary. She died on the morning of November 25.

CHAPTER NINE

End of the Peters Doll

Braile had been watching me closely. I met his questioning gaze, and tried to conceal the perturbation which the diary had aroused. I said:

'I never knew Walters had so imaginative a mind.'

He flushed and asked angrily: 'You think she was fictionizing?'

'Not fictionizing exactly. Observing a series of ordinary occurrences through the glamour of an active imagination would be a better way of putting it.'

He said, incredulously, 'You don't realize that what she has written is an authentic even though unconscious description of an amazing piece of hypnotism?'

'The possibility did occur to me,' I answered tartly. 'But I find no actual evidence to support it. I do perceive, however, that Walters was not so well balanced as I had supposed her. I do find evidence that she was surprisingly emotional; that in at least one of her visits to this Madame Mandilip she was plainly overwrought and in an extreme state of nervous instability. I refer to her most indiscreet discussion of the Peters case, after she had been warned by me, you will remember, to say nothing of it to anyone whatsoever.'

'I remember it so well,' he said, 'that when I came to that part of the diary I had no further doubt of the hypnotism. Nevertheless, go on.'

'In considering two possible causes for any action, it is desirable to accept the more reasonable,' I said, dryly. 'Consider the actual facts, Braile. Walters lays stress upon the odd conduct and warnings of the girl. She admits the girl is a neurotic. Well, the conduct she describes is exactly what we would expect from a neurotic. Walters is attracted by the dolls and goes in to price them, as anyone would. She is acting under no compulsion. She meets a woman whose physical characteristics stimulate her imagination – and arouse her emotionalism. She confides in her. This woman, evidently also of the emotional type, likes her and makes her a present of a doll. The woman is an artist; she sees in Walters a desirable model. She asks her to pose – still no compulsion and a natural request – and Walters does pose for her. The woman has her technique, like all artists, and part of it is to make skeletons for the framework of her dolls. A natural and intelligent procedure. The sight of the skeleton suggests death to Walters, and the suggestion of death brings up the image of Peters which has been powerfully impressed upon her imagination. She becomes momentarily hysterical – again evidence of her overwrought condition. She takes tea with the doll-maker and is accidentally scalded. Naturally this arouses the solicitude of her hostess and she dresses the scald with some unguent in whose efficacy she believes. And that is all. Where in this entirely commonplace sequence of events is there evidence that Walters was hypnotized? Finally, assuming that she was hypnotized, what evidence is there of motive?'

'She herself gave it,' he said – ' *"to make a doll of you, my dear!"* '

I had almost convinced myself by my argument, and this remark exasperated me.

'I suppose,' I said, 'you want me to believe that once

99

lured into the shop, Walters was impelled by occult arts to return until this Madame Mandilip's devilish purpose was accomplished. That the compassionate shop-girl tried to save her from what the old melodramas called a fate worse than death – although not precisely the fate they meant. That the doll she was to be given for her niece was the bait on the hook of a sorceress. That it was necessary she be wounded so the witch's salve could be applied. That it was the salve which carried the unknown death. That the first trap failing, the accident of the tea-kettle was contrived and was successful. And that now Walters' soul is fluttering inside the witch's mirror, just as she had dreamed. And all this, my dear Braile, is the most outrageous superstition!'

'Ah!' he said obliquely. 'So those possibilities did occur to you after all? Your mind is not so fossilized as a few moments ago I supposed.'

I became still more exasperated.

'It is your theory that from the moment Walters entered the store, every occurrence she has narrated was designed to give this Madame Mandilip possession of her soul, a design that was consummated by Walters' death?'

He hesitated, and then said: 'In essence – yes.'

'A soul!' I mused, sardonically. 'But I have never seen a soul. I know of no one whose evidence I would credit who has seen a soul. What is a soul – if it exists? It is a ponderable? Material? If your theory is correct it must be. How could one gain possession of something which is both imponderable and nonmaterial? How would one know one had it if it could not be seen nor weighed, felt nor measured, nor heard? If not material, how could it be constrained, directed, confined? As you suggest has been done with Walters' soul by this doll-maker. If material, then where does it reside in the body? Within the brain? I have operated upon hundreds and never yet have I opened any secret chamber housing this mysterious occupant. Little cells, far more complicated in their workings than any machinery ever devised, changing their possessor's mentality, moods, reason, emotion, personality – according to whether the little cells are functioning well or ill. These I have found, Braile – but never a soul. Surgeons have thoroughly explored the balance of the body. They, too, have found no secret temple within it. Show me a soul, Braile, and I'll believe in – Madame Mandilip.'

He studied me in silence for a little, then nodded.

'Now I understand. It's hit you pretty hard, too, hasn't it? You're doing a little beating of your own against the mirror, aren't you? Well, I've had a struggle to thrust aside what I've been taught is reality and to admit there may be something else just as real. This matter, Lowell, is extra-medical, outside the science we know. Until we admit that, we'll get nowhere. There are still two points I'd like to take up. Peters and the Darnley woman died the same kind of death. Ricori finds that they both had dealings with a Madame Mandilip – or so we can assume. He visits her and narrowly escapes death. Harriet visits her, and dies as Darnley and Peters did. Reasonably, therefore, doesn't all this point to Madame Mandilip as a possible source of the evil that overtook all four?'

'Certainly,' I answered.

'Then it must follow that there could have been real cause for the fear and forebodings of Harriet. That there *could* exist a cause other than emotionalism and

101

too much imagination – even though Harriet were unaware of these circumstances.'

Too late I realized the dilemma into which my admission had put me, but I could answer only in the
affirmative.

'The second point is her loss of all desire to return
to the doll-maker after the teapot incident. Did that
strike you as curious?'

'No. If she were emotionally unstable, the shock
would automatically set itself up as an inhibition, a
subconscious barrier. Unless they are masochists, such
types do not like to return to the scene of an unpleasant
experience.'

'Did you notice her remark that after the scalding,
the woman did not accompany her to the door of the
store? And that it was the first time she had neglected
to do so?'

'Not particularly. Why?'

'This. If the application of the salve constituted the
final act, and thereafter death became inevitable, it
might be highly embarrassing to Madame Mandilip to
have her victim going in and out of her shop during the
time it took the poison to kill. The seizure might even
take place there, and lead to dangerous questions. The
clever thing, therefore, would be to cause the unsus-
pecting sacrifice to lose all interest in her; indeed, feel a
repulsion against her, or even perhaps forget her. This
could be easily accomplished by post-hypnotic suggestion. And Madame Mandilip had every opportunity
for it. Would this not explain Harriet's distaste as
logically as imagination – or emotionalism?'

'Yes,' I admitted.

'And so,' he said, 'we have the woman's failure to
go to the door with Harriet that day explained. Her

102

plot has succeeded. It is all over. And she has planted her suggestion. No need now for any further contact with Harriet. She lets her go, unaccompanied. Significant symbolism of finality!'

He sat thinking.

'No need to meet Harriet again,' he half-whispered, ' 'til after death!'

I said, startled: 'What do you mean by that?'

'Never mind,' he answered.

He crossed to the charred spot upon the floor and picked up the heat-blasted crystals. They were about twice the size of olive pips and apparently of some composite. He walked to the table and looked down upon the grotesque figure with its skeleton ribs.

'Suppose the heat melted it?' he asked, and reached over to lift the skeleton. It held fast, and he gave it a sharp tug. There was a shrill twanging sound, and he dropped it with a startled oath. The thing fell to the floor. It writhed, the single wire of which it was made uncoiling.

Uncoiling, it glided over the floor like a serpent and came to rest, quivering.

We looked from it to the table.

The substance that had resembled a sprawling, flattened, headless body was gone. In its place was a film of fine gray dust which swirled and eddied for a moment in some unfelt draft – and then, too, was gone.

CHAPTER TEN

Nurse's Cap and Witch's Ladder

'She knows how to get rid of the evidence!'

Braile laughed – but there was no mirth in his laughter. I said nothing. It was the same thought I had held of McCann when the doll's head had vanished. But McCann could not be suspected of this. Evading any further discussion of the matter, we went to the Annex to see Ricori.

There were two new guards on watch at his door. They arose politely and spoke to us pleasantly. We entered softly. Ricori had slipped out of the drug into a natural sleep. He was breathing easily, peacefully, in deep and healing slumber.

His room was a quiet one at the rear, overlooking a little enclosed garden. Both my houses are old-fashioned, dating back to a more peaceful New York; sturdy vines of Virginia creepers climb up them both at front and back. I cautioned the nurse to maintain utmost quiet, arranging her light so that it would cast only the slightest gleam upon Ricori. Going out, I similarly cautioned the guards, telling them that their chief's speedy recovery might depend upon silence.

It was now after six. I asked Braile to stay for dinner, and afterward to drop in on my patients at the hospital and to call me up if he thought it worth while. I wanted to stay at home and await Ricori's awakening, should it occur.

We had almost finished dinner when the telephone rang. Braile answered.

'McCann,' he said. I went to the instrument.

'Hello, McCann. This is Dr. Lowell.'

'How's the boss?'

'Better, I'm expecting him to awaken any moment and to be able to talk,' I answered, and listened intently to catch whatever reaction he might betray to this news.

'That's great, Doc!' I could detect nothing but deepest satisfaction in his tones. 'Listen, Doc, I seen Mollie an' I got some news. Dropped round on her right after I left you. Found Gilmore – that's her husband – home, an' that gave me a break. Said I'd come in to ask her how she'd like a little ride. She was tickled an' we left Gil home with the kid—'

'Does she know of Peters' death?' I interrupted.

'Nope. An' I didn't tell her. Now listen. I told you Horty – What? Why Missus Darnley, Jim Wilson's gal. Yeah. Let me talk, will you? I told you Horty was nuts on Mollie's kid. Early last month Horty comes in with a swell doll for the kid. Also she's nursing a sore hand she says she gets at the same place she got the doll. The woman she gets the doll from gave it to her, she tells Mollie – What? No, gave her the doll, not the hand. Say, Doc, ain't I speaking clear? Yeah, she gets her hand hurt where she got the doll. That's what I said. The woman fixes it up for her. She gives her the doll for nothing, Horty tells Mollie, because she thought Horty was so pretty an' for posing for her. Yeah, posing for her, making a statue of her or something. That makes a hit with Horty because she don't hate herself an' she thinks this doll woman a lallapaloozer. Yeah, a lallapaloozer, a corker! Yeah.

'About a week later Tom – that's Peters – shows up

while Horty's there an' sees the doll. Tom's a mite jealous of Horty with the kid an' asks her where she got it. She tells him a Madame Mandilip, an' where, an' Tom he says as this is a gal-doll she needs company, so he'll go an' get a boy-doll. About a week after this Tom turns up with a boy-doll the lick-an'-split of Horty's. Mollie asks him if he pays as much for it as Horty. They ain't told him about Horty not paying nothing for it or posing. Mollie says Tom looks sort of sheepish but all he says is, well, he ain't gone broke on it. She's going to kid him by asking if the doll woman thinks he's so pretty she wants him to pose, but the kid sets up a whoop about the boy-doll an' she forgets it. Tom don't show up again till about the first of this month. He's got a bandage on his hand an' Mollie, kidding, asks him if he got it where he got the doll. He looks surprised an' says "yes, but how the hell did you know that?" Yeah – yeah, that's what she says he told her. What's that? Did the Mandilip woman bandage it for him? How the hell – I don't know. I guess so, maybe. Mollie didn't say an' I didn't ask. Listen, Doc, I told you Mollie's no dummy. What I'm tellin you took me two hours to get. Talking 'bout this, talking 'bout that an' coming back casual like to what I'm trying to find out. I'm afraid to ask too many questions. What? Oh, that's all right, Doc. No offense. Yeah, I think it pretty funny myself. But like I'm telling you I'm afraid to go too far. Mollie's too wise.

'Well, when Ricori comes up yesterday he uses the same tactics as me, I guess. Anyway, he admires the dolls an' asks her where she gets 'em an' how much they cost an' so on. Remember, I told you I stay out in the car while he's there. It's after that he goes home an' does the telephoning an' then beats it to the Mandi-

106

lip hag. Yeah, that's all. Does it mean anything? Yeah? All right then.'

He was silent for a moment or two, but I had not heard the click of the receiver. I asked:

'Are you there, McCann?'

'Yeah. I was just thinking.' His voice held a wistful note. 'I'd sure like to be with you when the boss comes to. But I'd best go down an' see how the hands are getting along with them two Mandilip cows. Maybe I'll call you up if it ain't too late. G'by.'

I walked slowly back to Braile, trying to marshal my disjointed thoughts. I repeated McCann's end of the conversation to him exactly. He did not interrupt me. When I had finished he said quietly:

'Hortense Darnley goes to the Mandilip woman, is given a doll, is asked to pose, is wounded there, is treated there. And dies. Peters goes to the Mandilip woman, gets a doll, is wounded there, is presumably treated there. And dies like Hortense. You see a doll for which, apparently, he has posed. Harriet goes through the same routine. And dies like Hortense and Peters. Now what?'

Suddenly I felt rather old and tired. It is not precisely stimulating to see crumbling what one has long believed to be a fairly well-ordered world of recognized cause and effect. I said wearily:

'I don't know.'

He arose, and patted my shoulder.

'Get some sleep. The nurse will call you if Ricori wakes. We'll get to the bottom of this thing.'

'Even if we fall to it,' I said, and smiled.

'Even if we have to fall to it,' he repeated, and did not smile.

After Braile had gone I sat for long, thinking. Then,

determined to dismiss my thoughts, I tried to read. I was too restless, and soon gave it up. Like the room in which Ricori lay, my study is at the rear, looking down upon the little garden. I walked to the window and stared out, unseeingly. More vivid than ever was that feeling of standing before a blank door which it was vitally important to open. I turned back into the study and was surprised to find it was close to ten o'clock. I dimmed my light and lay down upon the comfortable couch. Almost immediately I fell asleep.

I awoke from that sleep with a start, as though someone had spoken in my ear. I sat up, listening. There was utter silence around me. And suddenly I was aware that it was a strange silence, unfamiliar and oppressive. A thick, dead silence that filled the study and through which no sound from outside could penetrate. I jumped to my feet and turned on the lights, full. The silence retreated, seemed to pour out of the room like something tangible. But slowly. Now I could hear the ticking of my clock – ticking out abruptly, as though a silencing cover had been whisked from it. I shook my head impatiently, and walked to the window. I leaned out to breath the cool night air. I leaned out still more, so that I could see the window of Ricori's room, resting my hand on the trunk of the vine. I felt a tremor along it as though someone were gently shaking it – or as though some small animal were climbing it—

The window of Ricori's room broke into a square of light. Behind me I heard the shrilling of the Annex alarm bell which meant the urgent need of haste. I raced out of the study, and up the stairs and over.

As I ran into the corridor I saw that the guards were not at the door. The door was open. I stood stock-still on its threshold, incredulous—

One guard crouched beside the window, automatic in hand. The other knelt beside a body on the floor, his pistol pointed toward me. At her table sat the nurse, head bent upon her breast – unconscious or asleep. The bed was empty. The body on the floor was Ricori!

The guard lowered his gun. I dropped at Ricori's side. He was lying face down, stretched out a few feet from the bed. I turned him over. His face had the pallor of death, but his heart was beating.

'Help me lift him to the bed,' I said to the guard. 'Then shut that door.'

He did so, silently. The man at the window asked from the side of his mouth, never relaxing his watch outward:

'Boss dead?'

'Not quite,' I answered, then swore as I seldom do – 'What the hell kind of guards are you!'

The man who had shut the door gave a mirthless chuckle.

'There's more'n you goin' to ask that, Doc.'

I gave a glance at the nurse. She still sat huddled in the limp attitude of unconsciousness or deep sleep. I stripped Ricori of his pajamas and went over his body. There was no mark upon him. I sent for adrenalin, gave him an injection and went over to the nurse, and shook her. She did not awaken. I raised her eyelids. The pupils of her eyes were contracted. I flashed a light in them, without response. Her pulse and respiration were slow, but not dangerously so. I let her be for a moment and turned to the guards.

'What happened?'

They looked at each other uneasily. The guard at the window waved his hand as though bidding the other do the talking. This guard said:

'We're sitting out there. All at once the house gets damned still. I says to Jack there, "Sounds like they put a silencer on the dump." He says, "Yeah." We sit listening. Then all at once we hear a thump inside here. Like somebody falling out of bed. We crash the door. There's the boss like you seen him on the floor. There's the nurse asleep like you see her. We glim the alarm and pull it. Then we wait for somebody to come. That's all, ain't it, Jack?'

'Yeah,' answered the guard at the window, tonelessly. 'Yeah, I guess that's all.'

I looked at him, suspiciously.

'You guess that's all? What do you mean – you guess?'

Again they looked at each other.

'Better come clean, Bill,' said the guard at the window.

'Hell, he won't believe it,' said the other.

'And nobody else. Anyway, tell him.'

The guard Bill said:

'When we crash the door we seen something like a couple of cats fighting there beside the window. The boss is lying on the floor. We had our guns out but was afraid to shoot for what you told us. Then we heard a funny noise outside like somebody blowing a flute. The two things broke loose and jumped up on the window sill, and out. We jumped to the window. And we didn't see nothing.'

'You saw the things at the window. What did they look like then?' I asked.

'You tell him, Jack.'

'Dolls!'

A shiver went down my back. It was the answer I had expected – and dreaded. Out the window! I recalled the tremor of the vine when I gripped it! The guard who had closed the door looked at me, and I saw his jaw drop.

'Jesus, Jack!' he gasped. 'He believes it!'

I forced myself to speak.

'What kind of dolls?'

The guard at the window answered, more confidently.

'One we couldn't see well. The other looked like one of your nurses if she'd shrunk to about two feet!'

One of my nurses . . . Walters . . . I felt a wave of weakness and sank down on the edge of Ricori's bed.

Something white on the floor at the head of it caught my eye. I stared at it stupidly, then leaned and picked it up.

It was a nurse's cap, a little copy of those my nurses wear. It was about large enough to fit the head of a two foot doll . . .

There was something else where it had been. I picked that up.

It was a knotted cord of hair . . . pale ashen hair . . . with nine curious knots spaced at irregular intervals along it . . .

The guard named Bill stood looking down at me anxiously. He asked:

'Want me to call any of your people, Doc?'

'Try to get hold of McCann,' I bade him; then spoke to the other guard: 'Close the windows and fasten them and pull down the curtains. Then lock the door.'

Bill began to telephone. Stuffing the cap and knotted cord in my pocket, I walked over to the nurse. She was rapidly recovering and in a minute or two I had her awake. At first her eyes dwelt on me, puzzled; took in the lighted room and the two men, and the puzzlement changed to alarm. She sprang to her feet.

'I didn't see you come in! Did I fall asleep . . . what's happened? . . .' Her hand went to her throat.

'I'm hoping you can tell us,' I said, gently.

She stared at me uncomprehendingly. She said, confusedly:

'I don't know . . . it became terribly still . . . I thought I saw something moving at the window . . . then there was a queer fragrance . . . and then I looked up to see you bending over me.'

I asked: 'Can you remember anything of what you saw at the window? The least detail – the least impression. Please try.'

She answered, hesitantly: 'There was something white . . . I thought someone . . . something . . . was watching me . . . then came the fragrance, like flowers . . . that's all.'

Bill hung up the telephone: 'All right, Doc. They're after McCann. Now what?'

'Miss Butler,' I turned to the nurse. 'I'm going to relieve you for the balance of the night. Go to bed. And I want you to sleep. I prescribe—' I told her what.

'You're not angry – you don't think I've been careless—'

'No, to both.' I smiled and patted her shoulder. 'The case has taken an unexpected turn, that's all. Now don't ask any more questions.'

I walked with her to the door, opened it.

'Do exactly as I say.'

I closed and locked the door behind her.

I sat beside Ricori. The shock that he had experienced – whatever it might have been – should either cure or kill, I thought grimly. As I watched him, a

112

tremor went through his body. Slowly an arm began to lift, fist clenched. His lips moved. He spoke, in Italian and so swiftly that I could get no word. His arm fell back. I stood up from the bed. The paralysis had gone. He could move and speak. But would he be able to do so when consciousness assumed sway? I left this for the next few hours to decide I could do nothing else.

'Now listen to me carefully,' I said to the two guards. 'No matter how strange what I am going to say will seem, you must obey me in every detail – Ricori's life depends upon your doing so. I want one of you to sit close beside me at the table here. I want the other to sit beside Ricori, at the head of the bed and between him and me. If I am asleep and he should awaken, arouse me. If you see any change in his condition, immediately awaken me. Is that clear?'

They said: 'Okay.'

'Very well. Now here is the most important thing of all. You must watch *me* even more closely. Whichever of you sits beside me must not take his eyes off me. If I should go to your chief it would be to do one of three things only – listen to his heart and breathing – lift his eyelids – take his temperature. I mean, of course, if he should be as he now is. If I seem to awaken and attempt to do anything other than these three – stop me. If I resist, make me helpless – tie me up and gag me – no, don't gag me – listen to me and remember what I say. Then telephone to Dr. Braile – here is his number.'

I wrote, and passed it to them.

'Don't damage me any more than you can help,' I said, and laughed.

They stared at each other, plainly disconcerted.

'If you say so, Doc—' began the guard Bill, doubtfully.

113

'I do say so. Do not hesitate. If you should be wrong, I'll not hold it against you.'

'The Doc knows what he's about, Bill,' said the guard Jack.

'Okay then,' said Bill.

I turned out all the lights except that beside the nurse's table. I stretched myself in her chair and adjusted the lamp so my face could be plainly seen. That little white cap I had picked from the floor had shaken me – damnably! I drew it out and placed it in a drawer. The guard Jack took his station beside Ricori. Bill drew up a chair, and sat facing me. I thrust my hand into my pocket and clutched the knotted cord, closed my eyes, emptied my mind of all thought, and relaxed. In abandoning, at least temporarily, my conception of a sane universe I had determined to give that of Madame Mandilip's every chance to operate.

Faintly, I heard a clock strike one. I slept.

Somewhere a vast wind was roaring. It circled and swept down upon me. It bore me away. I knew that I had no body, that indeed I had no form. Yet *I was*. A formless sentience whirling in that vast wind. It carried me into infinite distance. Bodiless, intangible as I knew myself to be, yet it poured into me an unearthly vitality. I roared with the wind in unhuman jubilance. The vast wind circled and raced me back from immeasurable space. . . .

I seemed to awaken, that pulse of strange jubilance still surging through me. . . . Ah! There was what I must destroy . . . there on the bed . . . must kill so that this pulse of jubilance would not cease . . . must kill so that the vast wind would sweep me up again and away and feed me with its life . . . but careful . . . careful . . .

there – there in the throat just under the ear . . . there is where I must plunge it . . . then off with the wind again . . . there where the pulse beats . . . *what is holding me back?* . . . caution . . . caution. . . . *'I am going to take his temperature'* . . . that's it, careful. . . . *'I am going to take his temperature.'* . . . Now – one quick spring, then into his throat where the pulse beats. . . . *'Not with that you don't!'* . . . Who said that? . . . still holding me . . . rage, consuming and ruthless . . . blackness and the sound of a vast wind roaring away and away. . . .

I heard a voice: 'Slap him again, Bill, but not so hard. He's coming around.' I felt a stinging blow on my face. The dancing mists cleared from before my eyes. I was standing halfway between the nurse's table and Ricori's bed. The guard Jack held my arms pinioned to my sides. The guard Bill's hand was still raised. There was something clenched tightly in my own hand. I looked down. It was a strong scalpel, razor-edged!

I dropped the scalpel. I said, quietly: 'It's all right now, you can release me.'

The guard Bill said nothing. His comrade did not loose his grip. I twisted my head and I saw that both their faces were sallow white. I said:

'It was what I had expected. It was why I instructed you. It is over. You can keep your guns on me if you like.'

The guard who held me freed my arms. I touched my cheek gingerly. I said mildly:

'You must have hit me rather hard, Bill.'

He said: 'If you could a seen your face, Doc, you'd wonder I didn't smash it.'

I nodded, clearly sensible now of the demonic quality of that rage, I asked:

'What did I do?'

115

The guard Bill said: 'You wake up and set there for a minute staring at the chief. Then you take something out of that drawer and get up. You say you're going to take his temperature. You're half to him before we see what you got. I shout, "Not with that you don't!" Jack grabs you. Then you went – crazy. And I had to slam you. That's all.'

I nodded again. I took out of my pocket the knotted cord of woman's pale hair, held it over a dish and touched a match to it. It began to burn, writhing like a tiny snake as it did so, the complex knots untying as the flame touched them. I dropped the last inch of it upon the plate and watched it turn to ash.

'I think there'll be no more trouble to-night,' I said. 'But keep up your watch just as before.'

I dropped back into the chair and closed my eyes. . . .

Well, Braile had not shown me a soul, but – I believed in Madame Mandilip.

CHAPTER ELEVEN

A Doll Kills

The balance of the night I slept soundly and dreamlessly. I awakened at my usual hour of seven. The guards were alert. I asked if anything had been heard from McCann, and they answered no. I wondered a little at that, but they did not seem to think it out of the ordinary. Their reliefs were soon due, and I cautioned them to speak to no one but McCann about the occurrences of the night, reminding them that no one would be likely to believe them if they did. They assured me, earnestly, that they would be silent. I told them that I wanted the guards to remain within the room thereafter, as long as they were necessary.

Examining Ricori, I found him sleeping deeply and naturally. In all ways his condition was most satisfactory. I concluded that the second shock, as sometimes happens, had counteracted the lingering effects of the initial one. When he awakened, he would be able to speak and move. I gave this reassuring news to the guards. I could see that they were bursting with questions. I gave them no encouragement to ask them.

At eight, my day nurse for Ricori appeared, plainly much surprised to have found Butler sleeping and to find me taking her place. I made no explanation, simply telling her that the guards would now be stationed within the room instead of outside the door.

At eight-thirty, Braile dropped in on me for breakfast, and to report. I let him finish before I apprised him

117

of what had happened. I said nothing, however, of the nurse's little cap, nor of my own experience.

I assumed this reticence for well-considered reasons. One, Braile would accept in its entirety the appalling deduction from the cap's presence. I strongly suspected that he had been in love with Walters, and that I would be unable to restrain him from visiting the doll-maker. Usually hard-headed, he was in this matter far too suggestible. It would be dangerous for him, and his observations would be worthless to me. Second, if he knew of my own experience, he would without doubt refuse to let me out of his sight. Third – either of these contingencies would defeat my own purpose alone – with the exception of McCann to keep watch outside the shop.

What would come of that meeting I could not forecast. But, obviously, it was the only way to retain my self-respect. To admit that what had occurred was witchcraft, sorcery, supernatural – was to surrender to superstition. Nothing can be supernatural. If anything exists, it must exist in obedience to natural laws. Material bodies *must* obey material laws. We may not know those laws – but they exist nevertheless. If Madame Mandilip possessed knowledge of an unknown science, it behooved me as an exemplar of known science, to find out what I could about the other. Especially as I had recently responded so thoroughly to it. That I had been able to outguess her in her technique – if it had been that, and not a self-induced illusion – gave me a pleasant feeling of confidence. At any rate, meet her I must.

It happened to be one of my days for consultation, so I could not get away until after two. I asked Braile to take charge of matters after that, for a few hours.

Close to ten the nurse telephoned that Ricori was awake, that he was able to speak and had been asking for me.

He smiled at me as I entered the room. As I leaned over and took his wrist he said:

'I think you have saved more than my life, Dr. Lowell! Ricori thanks you. He will never forget!'

A bit florid, but thoroughly in character. It showed that his mind was functioning normally. I was relieved.

'We'll have you up in a jiffy.' I patted his hand. He whispered: 'Have there been any more – deaths?'

I had been wondering whither he had retained any recollection of the affair of the night. I answered:

'No. But you have lost much strength since McCann brought you here. I don't want you to do much talking to-day.' I added, casually: 'No, nothing has happened. Oh, yes – you fell out of bed this morning. Do you remember?'

He glanced at the guards and then back at me. He said:

'I am weak. Very weak. You must make me strong quickly.'

'We'll have you sitting up in two days, Ricori.'

'In less than two days I must be up and out. There is a thing I must do. It cannot wait.'

I did not want him to become excited. I abandoned any intention of asking what had happened in the car. I said, incisively:

'That will depend entirely upon you. You must not excite yourself. You must do as I tell you. I am going to leave you now, to give orders for your nutrition. Also, I want your guards to remain in this room.'

He said: 'And still you tell me – nothing has happened.'

'I don't intend to have anything happen.' I leaned over him and whispered: 'McCann has guards around the Mandilip woman. She cannot run away.'

He said: 'But her servitors are more efficient than mine, Dr Lowell!'

I looked at him sharply. His eyes were inscrutable. I went back to my office, deep in thought. What did Ricori know?

At eleven o'clock McCann called me on the telephone. I was so glad to hear from him that I was angry.

'Where on earth have you been—' I began.

'Listen, Doc. I'm at Mollie's – Peter's sister,' he interrupted. 'Come here quick.'

The peremptory demand added to my irritation.

'Not now,' I answered. 'There are my office hours. I will not be free until two.'

'Can't you break away? Something's happened. I don't know what to do!' There was desperation in his voice.

'*What* has happened?' I asked.

'I can't tell you over—' His voice steadied, grew gentle; I heard him say, *'Be quiet, Mollie. It can't do no good!'* Then to me – 'Well, come as soon as you can, Doc. I'll wait. Take the address.' Then when he had given it to me, I heard him again speaking to another – *'Quit it, Mollie! I ain't going to leave you.'*

He hung up, abruptly. I went back to my chair, troubled. He had not asked me about Ricori. That in itself was disquieting. Mollie? Peters' sister, of course! Was it that she had learned of her brother's death, and suffered collapse? I recalled that Ricori had said she was soon to be a mother. No, I felt that McCann's panic had been due to something more than that. I became more and more uneasy. I looked over my appointments.

There were no important ones. Coming to sudden determination, I told my secretary to call up and postpone them. I ordered my car, and set out for the address McCann had given me.

McCann met me at the door of the apartment. His face was drawn and his eyes haunted. He drew me within without a word, and led me through the hall. I passed an open door and glimpsed a woman with a sobbing child in her arms. He took me into a bedroom and pointed to the bed.

There was a man lying on it, covers pulled up to his chin. I went over to him, looked down upon him, touched him. The man was dead. He had been dead for hours. McCann said:

'Mollie's husband. Look him over like you done the boss.'

I had a curiously unpleasant sense of being turned on a potter's wheel by some inexorable hand – from Peters, to Walters, to Ricori, to the body before me . . . would the wheel stop there?

I stripped the dead man. I took from my bag a magnifying glass and probes. I went over the body inch by inch, beginning at the region of the heart. Nothing there . . . nothing anywhere . . . I turned the body over. . . .

At once, at the base of the skull, I saw a minute puncture.

I took a fine probe and inserted it. The probe – and again I had that feeling of infinite repetition – slipped into the puncture. I manipulated it, gently.

Something like a long thin needle had been thrust into that vital spot just where the spinal cord connects with the brain. By accident, or perhaps because the needle had been twisted savagely to tear the nerve paths, there had been paralysis of respiration and almost instant death.

I withdrew the probe and turned to McCann.

'This man has been murdered,' I said. 'Killed by the same kind of weapon with which Ricori was attacked. But whoever did it made a better job. He'll never come to life again – as Ricori did.'

'Yeah?' said McCann, quietly. 'An' me an' Paul was the only ones with Ricori when it happened. An' the only ones here with this man, Doc, was his wife an' baby! Now what're you going to do about that? Say those two put him on the spot – like you thought we done the boss?'

I said: 'What do you know about this, McCann? And how did you come to be here so – opportunely?'

He answered, patiently: 'I wasn't here when he was killed – if that's what you're getting at. If you want to know the time, it was two o'clock. Mollie got me on the 'phone about an hour ago an' I come straight up.'

'She had better luck than I had,' I said dryly. 'Ricori's people have been trying to get hold of you since one o'clock last night.'

'I know. But I didn't know it till just before Mollie called me. I was on my way to see you. An' if you want to know what I was doing all night, I'll tell you. I was out on the boss's business, an' yours. For one thing trying to find out where that hell-cat niece keeps her coupé. I found out – too late.'

'But the men who we're supposed to be watching . . .'

'Listen, Doc, won't you talk to Mollie now?' he interrupted me, 'I'm afraid for her. It's only what I told her about you an' that you was coming that's kept her up.'

'Take me to her,' I said, abruptly.

We went into the room where I had seen the woman

122

and the sobbing child. The woman was not more than twenty-seven or -eight, I judged, and in ordinary circumstances would have been unusually attractive. Now her face was drawn and bloodless, in her eyes horror, and a fear on the very borderline of madness. She stared at me, vacantly; she kept rubbing her lips with the tips of her forefingers, staring at me with those eyes out of which looked a mind emptied of everything but fear and grief. The child, a girl of four, kept up her incessant sobbing. McCann shook the woman by the shoulder.

'Snap out of it, Mollie,' he said, roughly, but pityingly, too. 'Here's the Doc.'

The woman became aware of me, abruptly. She looked at me steadily for slow moments, then asked, less like one questioning than one relinquishing a last thin thread of hope:

'He is dead?'

She read the answer in my face. She cried:

'Oh, Johnnie – Johnnie Boy! Dead!'

She took the child up in her arms. She said to it, almost tranquilly: 'Johnnie Boy has gone away, darling. Daddy has had to go away. Don't cry, darling, we'll soon see him!'

I wished she would break down, weep; but that deep fear which never left her eyes was too strong; it blocked all normal outlets of sorrow. Not much longer, I realized, could her mind stand up under that tension.

'McCann,' I whispered, 'say something, do something to her that will arouse her. Make her violently angry, or make her cry. I don't care which.'

He nodded. He snatched the child from her arms and thrust it behind him. He leaned, his face close to the woman's. He said, brutally:

'Come clean, Mollie! Why did you kill John?'

For a moment the woman stood, uncomprehending. Then a tremor shook her. The fear vanished from her eyes and fury took its place. She threw herself upon McCann, fists beating at his face. He caught her, pinioned her arms. The child screamed.

The woman's body relaxed, her arms fell to her sides. She crumpled to the floor, her head bent over her knees. And tears came. McCann would have lifted, comforted her. I stopped him.

'Let her cry. It's the best thing for her.'

And after a little while she looked up at McCann and said, shakily:

'You didn't mean that, Dan?'

He said: 'No, I know you didn't do it, Mollie. But now you've got to talk to the Doc. There's a lot to be done.'

She asked, normally enough now: 'Do you want to question me, Doctor? Or shall I just go on and tell you what happened?'

McCann said: 'Tell him the way you told me. Begin with the doll.'

I said: 'That's right. You tell me your story. If I've any questions, I'll ask them when you are done.'

She began:

'Yesterday afternoon Dan, here, came and took me out for a ride. Usually John does not . . . did not . . . get home until about six. But yesterday he was worried about me and came home early, around three. He likes . . . he liked . . . Dan, and urged me to go. It was a little after six when I returned.

' "A present came for the kid while you were out, Mollie," he said. "It's another doll. I'll bet Tom sent it." Tom is my brother.

124

'There was a big box on the table, and I lifted the lid. In it was the most life-like doll imaginable. A perfect thing. A little girl-doll. Not a baby-doll, but a doll like a child about ten or twelve years old. Dressed like a schoolgirl, with her books strapped, and over her shoulder – only about a foot high, but perfect. The sweetest face – a face like a little angel!

'John said: "It was addressed to you, Molie, but I thought it was flowers and opened it. Looks as though it could talk, doesn't it? I'll bet it's what they call a portrait-doll. Some kid posed for that, all right."

'At that, I was sure Tom had sent it, because he had given little Mollie one doll before, and a friend of mine who's . . . whose dead . . . gave her one from the same place, and she told me the woman who made the dolls had gotten her to pose for one. So putting this together, I knew Tom had gone and gotten little Mollie another. But I asked John: "Wasn't there a note or a card or anything in it?" He said, "No – oh, yes, there was one funny thing. Where is it? I must have stuck it in my pocket."

'He hunted around in his pockets and brought out a cord. It had knots in it, and it looked as if it was made of hair. I said, "Wonder what Tom's idea was in that?" John put it back in his pocket, and I thought nothing more about it.

'Little Mollie was asleep. We put the doll beside her where she could see it when she woke up. When she did, she was in raptures over it. We had dinner, and Mollie played with the doll. After we put her to bed I wanted to take it away from her, but she cried so we let her go to sleep with it. We played cards until eleven, and then made ready for bed.

'Mollie is apt to be restless, and she still sleeps in a

125

low crib – so she can't fall out. The crib is in our bedroom, in the corner beside one of the two windows. Between the two windows is my dressing table, and our bed is set with its head against the wall opposite the windows. We both stopped and looked at Mollie, as we always do . . . did. She was sound asleep with the doll clasped in one arm, its head on her shoulder.

'John said: "Lord, Mollie – that doll looks as alive as the baby! You wouldn't be surprised to see it get up and walk. Whoever posed for it was some sweet kid."

'And that was true. It had the sweetest, gentlest little face . . . and oh, Dr Lowell . . . that's what helps make it so dreadful . . . so utterly dreadful. . . .'

I saw the fear begin to creep back into her eyes.

McCann said: 'Buck up, Mollie!'

'I tried to take the doll. It was so lovely I was afraid the baby might roll on it or damage it some way,' she went on, again quietly but she held it fast, and I did not want to awaken her. So I let it be. While we were undressing, John took the knotted cord out of his pocket.

' "That's a funny looking bunch of knots," he said. "When you hear from Tom ask him what it's for." He tossed the cord on the little table at his side of the bed. It wasn't long before he was asleep. And then I went asleep too—

'And then I woke up . . . or thought I did . . . for if I was awake or dreaming I don't know. It must have been a dream – and yet . . . Oh God . . . John is dead . . . I heard him die. . . .'

Again, for a little time, the tears flowed. Then:

'If I was awake, it must have been the stillness that awakened me. And yet – it is what makes me feel I must have been dreaming. There couldn't be such silence . . . except in a dream. We are on the second floor, and

126

always there is some sound from the street. There wasn't the least sound now . . . it was as though . . . as though the whole world had suddenly been stricken dumb. I thought I sat up, listening . . . listening thirstily for the tiniest noises. I could not even hear John breathing. I was frightened, for there was something dreadful in that stillness. Something – living! Something – wicked! I tried to lean over to John, tried to touch him, to awaken him.

'I could not move! I could not stir a finger! I tried to speak, to cry out. I could not!

'The window curtains were partly drawn. A faint light showed beneath and around them from the street. Suddenly this was blotted out. The room was dark – utterly dark.

'And then the green glow began—

'At first it was the dimmest gleam. It did not come from outside. It was in the room itself. It would flicker and dim, flicker and dim. But always after each dimming it was brighter. It was green – like the light of the firefly. Or like looking at moonlight through clear green water. At last the green glow became steady. It was like light, and still it wasn't light. It wasn't brilliant. It was just glowing. And it was everywhere – under the dressing table, under the chairs . . . I mean it cast no shadows. I could see everything in the bedroom. I could see the baby asleep in her crib, the doll's head on her shoulder. . . .

'*The doll moved!*

'It turned its head, and seemed to listen to the baby's breathing. It put its little hands upon the baby's arm. The arm dropped away from it. . . .

'*The doll sat up!*

'And now I was sure that I must be dreaming . . .

the strange silence . . . the strange green glow . . . and this . . .

'The doll clambered over the side of the crib, and dropped to the floor. It came skipping over the floor toward the bed like a child, swinging its school books by their strap. It turned its head from side to side as it came, looking around the room like a curious child. It caught sight of the dressing table, and stopped, looking up at the mirror. It climbed up the chair in front of the dressing table. It jumped from the chair to the table, tossed its books aside and began to admire itself in the mirror.

'It preened itself. It turned and looked at itself, first over this shoulder and then over that. I thought: "What a queer fantastic dream!" It thrust its face close to the mirror and rearranged and patted its hair. I thought: "What a vain little doll!" And then I thought: "I'm dreaming all this because John said the doll was so lifelike he wouldn't be surprised to see it walk." And then I thought: "But I can't be dreaming, or I wouldn't be trying to account for what I'm dreaming!" And then it all seemed so absurd that I laughed. I knew I had made no sound. I knew I couldn't . . . that the laugh was inside me. But it was as though the doll had heard me. It turned and looked straight at me—

'My heart seemed to die within me. I've had nightmares, Dr Lowell – but never in the worst of them did I feel as I did when the doll's eyes met mine. . . .

'They were the eyes of a devil!

'They shone red. I mean they were – were – luminous . . . like some animal's eyes in the dark. But it was the – the – the *hellishness* in them that made me feel as though a hand had gripped my heart! Those eyes from hell in that face like one of God's own angels. . . .

'I don't know how long it stood there, glaring at me. But at last it swung itself down and sat on the edge of the dressing table, legs swinging like a child's and still with its eyes on mine. Then slowly, deliberately, it lifted its little arm and reached behind its neck. Just as slowly it brought its arm back. In its hand was a long pin . . . like a dagger. . . .

'It dropped from the dressing table to the floor. It skipped toward me and was hidden by the bottom of the bed. An instant – and it had clambered up the bed and stood, still looking at me with those red eyes, at John's feet.

'I tried to cry out, tried to move, tried to arouse John. I prayed – *"Oh God, wake him up! Dear God – wake him!"* . . .

'The doll looked away from me. It stood there, looking at John. It began to creep along his body, up toward his head. I tried to move my hand, to follow it. I could not. The doll passed out of my sight. . . .

'I heard a dreadful, sobbing groan. I felt John shudder, then stretch and twist. . . . I heard him sigh. . . .

'Deep . . . deep down. . . . I knew John was dying . . . and I could do nothing . . . in the silence . . . in the green glow. . . .

'I heard something like the note of a flute, from the street, beyond the windows. There was a tiny scurrying. I saw the doll skip across the floor and spring up to the window sill. It knelt there for a moment, looking out into the street. It held something in its hand. And then I saw that what it held was the knotted cord John had thrown on his table.

'I heard the flute note again . . . the doll swung itself out of the window. . . . I had a glimpse of its red eyes.

. . . I saw its little hands clutching the sill . . . and it was gone. . . .

'The green glow . . . blinked and . . . went out. The light from the street returned around the curtains. The silence seemed . . . seemed . . . to be *sucked* away.

'And then something like a wave of darkness swept over me. I went down under it. Before it swept over me I heard the clock strike two.

'When I awakened again . . . or came out of my faint . . . or, if it was just a dream, when I awakened . . . I turned to John. He lay there . . . so still! I touched him . . . he was cold . . . so cold!

'I knew he was dead!

'Dr Lowell . . . tell me . . . what was dream and what was real? I know that no doll could have killed John!

'Did he reach out to me when he was dying, and did the dream come from that? Or did I . . . dreaming . . . kill him?'

CHAPTER TWELVE

Technique of Madame Mandilip

There was an agony in her eyes that forbade the truth, so I lied to her.

'I can comfort you as to that, at least. Your husband died of entirely natural causes – from a blood clot in the brain. My examination satisfied me thoroughly as to that. You had nothing to do with it. As for the doll – you had an unusually vivid dream, that is all.'

She looked at me as one who would give her soul to believe. She said:

'But I heard him die!'

'It is quite possible—' I plunged into a somewhat technical explanation which I knew she would not quite understand, but would, perhaps, be therefore convincing – 'You may have been half-awake – on what we term the borderline of waking consciousness. In all probability the entire dream was suggested by what you heard. Your subconsciousness tried to explain the sounds, and conceived the whole fantastic drama you have recited to me. What seemed, in your dream, to take up many minutes actually passed through your mind in a split second – the subconsciousness makes its own time. It is a common experience. A door slams, or there is some other abrupt and violent sound. It awakens the sleeper. When he is fully awake he has recollection of some singularly vivid dream which ended with a loud noise. In reality, his dream began with the noise. The dream may have seemed to him to

131

have taken hours. It was, in fact, almost instantaneous, taking place in the brief moment between noise and awakening.'

She drew a deep breath; her eyes lost some of their agony. I pressed my advantage.

'And there is another thing you must remember – your condition. It makes many women peculiarly subject to realistic dreams, usually of an unpleasant character. Sometimes even to – hallucinations.'

She whispered: 'That is true. When little Mollie was coming I had the most dreadful dreams—'

She hesitated; I saw doubt again cloud her face.

'But the doll – the doll is gone!' she said.

I cursed to myself at that, caught unawares and with no ready answer. But McCann had one. He said, easily:

'Sure it's gone, Mollie. I dropped it down the chute into the waste. After what you told me I thought you'd better not see it any more.'

She asked, sharply:

'Where did you find it? I looked for it.'

'Guess you weren't in shape to do much looking,' he answered. 'I found it down at the foot of the kid's crib, all messed up in the covers. It was busted. Looked like the kid had been dancing on it in her sleep.'

She said, hesitantly: 'It might have slipped down. I don't think I looked there—'

I said, severely, so she might not suspect collusion between McCann and myself:

'You ought not to have done that, McCann. If you had shown the doll to her, Mrs Gilmore would have known at once that she had been dreaming and she would have been spared much pain.'

'Well, I ain't a doctor.' His voice was sullen. 'I done what I thought best.'

'Go down and see if you can find it,' I ordered, tartly. He glanced at me sharply. I nodded – and hoped he understood. In a few minutes he returned.

'They cleaned out the waste only fifteen minutes ago,' he reported, lugubriously. 'The doll went with it. I found this, though.'

He held up a little strap from which dangled a half-dozen miniature books. He asked:

'Was them what you dreamed the doll dropped on the dressing table, Mollie?'

She stared, and shrank away.

'Yes,' she whispered. 'Please put it away, Dan. I don't want to see it.'

He looked at me, triumphantly.

'I guess maybe I was right at that when I threw the doll away, Doc.'

I said: 'At any rate, now that Mrs. Gilmore is satisfied it was all a dream, there's no harm done.

'And now,' I took her cold hands in mine. 'I'm going to prescribe for you. I don't want to stay in this place a moment longer than you can help. I want you to pack a bag with whatever you and little Mollie may need for a week or so, and leave at once. I am thinking of your condition – and a little life that is on its way. I will attend to all the necessary formalities. You can instruct McCann as to – the other details. But I want you to go. Will you do this?'

To my relief, she assented readily. There was a somewhat harrowing moment when she and the child bade farewell to the body. But before many minutes she was on her way with McCann to relations. The child had wanted to take 'the boy and girl dolls.' I had refused to allow this, even at the risk of again arousing the mother's suspicions. I wanted nothing of Madame

133

Mandilip to accompany them to their refuge. McCann supported me, and the dolls were left behind.

I called an undertaker whom I knew. I made a last examination of the body. The minute puncture would not be noticed, I was sure. There was no danger of an autopsy, since my certification of the cause of death would not be questioned. When the undertaker arrived I explained the absence of the wife – imminent maternity and departure at my order. I set down the cause of death as thrombosis – rather grimly as I recalled the similar diagnosis of the banker's physician, and what I had thought of it.

After the body had been taken away, and as I sat waiting for McCann to return, I tried to orient myself to this phantasmagoria through which, it seemed to me, I had been moving for endless time. I tried to divest my mind of all prejudice, all preconceived ideas of what could and could not be. I began by conceding that this Madame Mandilip might possess some wisdom of which modern science is ignorant. I refused to call it witchcraft or sorcery. The words mean nothing, since they have been applied through the ages to entirely natural phenomena whose causes were not understood by the laity. Not so long ago, for example, the lighting of a match was 'witchcraft' to many savage tribes.

No, Madame Mandilip was no 'witch', as Ricori thought her. She was mistress of some unknown science – that was all.

And being a science, it must be governed by fixed laws – unknown though those laws might be to me. If the doll-maker's activties defied cause and effect, as I conceived them, still they must conform to laws of cause and effect of their own. There was nothing supernatural about them – it was only that, like the savages,

I did not know what made the match burn. Something of these laws, something of the woman's technique – using the word as signifying the details, collectively considered, of mechanical performance in any art – I thought I perceived. The knotted cord, 'the witch's ladder,' apparently was an essential in the animation of the dolls. One had been slipped into Ricori's pocket before the first attack upon him. I had found another beside his bed after the disturbing occurrences of the night. I had gone to sleep holding one of the cords – and had tried to murder my patient! A third cord had accompanied the doll that had killed John Gilmore.

Clearly, then, the cord was a part of the formula for the direction of control of the dolls.

Against this, was the fact that the intoxicated stroller could not have been carrying one of the 'ladders' when attacked by the Peters doll.

It might be, however, that the cord had only to do with the initial activity of the puppets; that once activated, their action might continue for an indefinite period.

There was evidence of a fixed formula in the making of the dolls. First, it seemed, the prospective victim's free consent to serve as model must be obtained; second, a wound which gave the opportunity to apply the salve which caused the unknown death; third, the doll must be a faithful replica of the victim. That the agency of death was the same in each case was proven by the similar symptoms.

But did those deaths actually have anything to do with the motility of the dolls? Were they actually a necessary part of the operation?

The doll-maker might believe so; indeed, undoubtedly did believe so.

I did not.

That the doll which had stabbed Ricori had been made in the semblance of Peters; that the 'nurse doll' which the guards had seen poised on my window-ledge might have been the one for which Walters had posed; that the doll which had thrust the pin into Gilmore's brain was, perhaps, the replica of little Anita, the eleven-year-old schoolgirl – all this I admitted.

But that anything of Peters, anything of Walters, anything of Anita had animated these dolls . . . that dying, something of their vitality, their minds, their 'souls' had been drawn from them, had been transmuted into an essence of evil, and imprisoned in these wire-skeletoned puppets . . . against this all my reason revolted. I could not force my mind to accept even the possibility.

My analysis was interrupted by the return of McCann.

He said, laconically : 'Well, we put it over.'

I asked. 'McCann – you weren't by any chance telling the truth when you said you found the doll?'

'No, Doc. The doll was gone all right.'

'But where did you get the little books?'

'Just where Mollie said the doll tossed 'em – on her dressing table. I snaked 'em after she'd told me her story. She hadn't noticed 'em. I had a hunch. It was a good one, wasn't it?'

'You had me wondering,' I replied. 'I don't know what we could have said if she had asked for the knotted cord.'

The cord didn't seem to make much of a dent on her—' He hesitated. 'But I think it means a hell of a lot, Doc. I think if I hadn't took her out, and John hadn't happened home, and Mollie had opened the box instead of him – I think it's Mollie he'd have found lying dead beside him.

'You mean—'

'I mean the dolls go for whichever gets the cords,' he said somberly.

Well, it was much the same thought I had in my own mind.

I asked: 'But why should anybody want to kill Mollie?'

'Maybe somebody thinks she knows too much. And that brings me to what I've been wanting to tell you. The Mandilip hag knows she's being watched!'

'Well, her watchers are better than ours.' I echoed Ricori; and I told McCann then of the second attack in the night; and why I had sought him.

'An' that,' he said when I had ended, 'proves the Mandilip hag knows who's behind the watch on her. She tried to wipe out both the boss and Mollie. She's onto us, Doc.'

'The dolls are accompanied,' I said. 'The musical note is a summons. They do not disappear into thin air. They answer the note and make their way . . . somehow . . . to whoever sounds the note. The dolls must be taken from the shop. Therefore one of the two women must take them. How did they evade your watchers?'

'I don't know.' The lean face was worried. 'The fish-white gal does it. Let me tell you what I found out, Doc. After I left you last night I go down to see what the boys have to say. I hear plenty. They say about four o'clock the gal goes in the back an' the old woman takes a chair in the store. They don't think nothing of that. But about seven who do they see walking down the street and into the doll joint but the gal. They give the boys in the back hell. But they ain't seen her go, an' they pass the buck to the boys in front.

'Then about eleven o'clock one of the relief lads

137

comes in with worse news. He says he's down at the foot of Broadway when a coupé turns the corner an' driving it is the gal. He can't be mistaken because he's seen her in the doll joint. She goes up Broadway at a clip. He sees there ain't nobody trailing her, an' he looks around for a taxi. Course there's nothing in sight – not even a parked car he can lift. So he comes down to the gang to ask what the hell they mean by it. An' again nobody's seen the gal go.

'I take a couple of the boys an' we start out to comb the neighborhood to find out where she stables the coupé. We don't have no luck at all until about four o'clock when one of the tails – one of the lads who's been looking – meets up with me. He says that about three he sees the gal – at least he thinks it's the gal – walking along the street around the corner from the joint. She's got a coupla big suitcases but they don't seem to trouble her none. She's walking quick. But *away* from the doll joint. He eases over to get a better look, when all of a sudden she ain't there. He sniffs around the place he's seen her. There ain't hide or hair of her. It's pretty dark, an' he tries the doors an' the areaways, but the doors are locked an' there ain't nobody in the areaways. So he gives it up an' hunts me.

'I look over the place. It's about a third down the block around the corner from the doll joint. The doll joint is eight numbers from the corner. They're mostly shops an' I guess storage up above. Not many people living there. The houses all old ones. Still, I don't see how the gal can get to the doll joint. I think maybe the tail's mistaken. He's seen somebody else, or just thinks he's seen somebody. But we scout close around, an' after a while we see a place that looks like it might stable a car. It don't take us long to open the doors. An' sure enough, there's a coupé with its engine still hot. It ain't been in long. Also it's the same kind of coupé the lad who's seen the gal says she was driving.

'I lock the place up again, an' go back to the boys. I watch with 'em the rest of the night. Not a light in the doll joint. But nigh eight o'clock, the gal shows up inside the shop and opens up!'

'Still,' I said at this point, 'you have no real evidence she had been out. The girl your man thought he saw might not have been she at all.'

He looked at me pityingly.

'She got out in the afternoon without 'em seeing her, didn't she? What's to keep her from doing the same thing at night? The lad saw her driving a coupé, didn't he? An' we find a coupé like it close where the wench dropped out of sight.'

I sat thinking. There was no reason to disbelieve McCann. And there was a sinister coincidence in the hours the girl had been seen. I said, half-aloud:

'The time she was out in the afternoon coincides with the time the doll was left at the Gilmores'. The time she was out at night coincides with the time of the attack upon Ricori, and the death of John Gilmore.'

'You hit it plumb in the eye!' said McCann. 'She goes an' leaves the dolls at Mollie's, an' comes back. She goes an' sets the dolls on the boss. She waits for 'em to pop out. Then she goes an' collects the one she's left at Mollie's. Then she beats it back home. They're in the suitcases she's carrying.'

I could not hold back the irritation of helpless mystification that swept me.

'And I suppose you think she got out of the house

139

by riding a broomstick up the chimney,' I said, sarcastically.

'No,' he answered, seriously. 'No, I don't, Doc. But them houses are old, and I think maybe there's a rat hole of a passage or something she gets through. Anyway, the hands are watching the street an' the coupé stable now, an' she can't pull that again.

He added, morosely:

'At that, I ain't saying she couldn't bridle a broomstick if she had to.'

I said, abruptly: 'McCann, I'm going down to talk to this Madame Mandilip. I want you to come with me.

He said: 'I'll be right beside you, Doc. With my fingers on my guns.'

I said: 'No, I'm going to see her alone. But I want you to keep close watch outside.'

He did not like that; argued; at last reluctantly assented.

I called up my office. I talked to Braile and learned that Ricori was recovering with astonishing rapidity. asked Braile to look after things the balance of the day, inventing a consultation to account for the request. I had myself switched to Ricori's room. I had the nurse tell him that McCann was with me, that we were making an investigation along a certain line, the results of which I would inform him on my return, and that, unless Ricori objected, I wanted McCann to stay with me the balance of the afternoon.

Ricori sent back word that McCann should follow my orders as though they were his own. He wanted to speak to me, but that I did not want. Pleading urgent haste, I rang off.

I ate an excellent and hearty lunch. I felt that it would help me hold tighter to the realities – or what I thought

140

were the realities – when I met this apparent mistress of illusions. McCann was oddly silent and preoccupied.

The clock was striking three when I set off to meet Madame Mandilip.

CHAPTER THIRTEEN

Madame Mandilip

I stood at the window of the doll-maker's shop, mastering a stubborn revulsion against entering. I knew McCann was on guard. I knew that Ricori's men were watching from the houses opposite, that others moved among the passers-by. Despite the roaring clatter of the elevated trains, the bustle of traffic along the Battery, the outwardly normal life of the street, the doll-maker's shop was a beleaguered fortress. I stood, shivering on its threshold, as though at the door of an unknown world.

There were only a few dolls displayed in the window, but they were unusual enough to catch the eyes of a child or a grown-up. Not so beautiful as that which had been given Walters, nor those two I had seen at the Gilmores', but admirable lures, nevertheless. The light inside the shop was subdued. I could see a slender girl moving at a counter. The niece of Madame Mandilip, no doubt. Certainly the size of the shop did not promise any such noble chamber behind it as Walters had painted in her diary. Still, the houses were old, and the back might extend beyond the limits of the shop itself—

Abruptly and impatiently I ceased to temporize. I opened the door and walked in.

The girl turned as I entered. She watched me as I came toward the counter. She did not speak. I studied her, swiftly. An hysterical type, obviously; one of the most perfect I had ever seen. I took note of the prominent pale blue eyes and with vague gaze and distended pupils; the long and slender neck and slightly rounded features; the pallor and the long thin fingers. Her hands were clasped, and I could see that these were unusually flexible – thus carrying out to the last jot the Laignel-Lavastine syndrome of the hysteric. In another time and other circumstances she would have been a priestess, voicing oracles, or a saint.

Fear was her handmaiden. There could be no doubt of that. And yet I was sure it was not of me she was frightened. Rather was it some deep and alien fear which lay coiled at the roots of her being, sapping her vitality – a spiritual fear. I looked at her hair. It was a silvery ash . . . the color . . . the color of the hair that formed the knotted cords!

As she saw me staring at her hair, the vagueness in her pale eyes diminished, was replaced by alertness. For the first time she seemed to be aware of me. I said, with the utmost casualness:

'I was attracted by the dolls in your window. I have a little granddaughter who would like one I think.'

'The dolls are for sale. If there is one you fancy, you may buy it. At its price.'

Her voice was low-pitched, almost whispering, indifferent. But I thought the intentness in her eyes sharpened.

'I suppose,' I answered, feigning something of irritation, 'that is what any chance customer may do. But it happens that this child is a favorite of mine and for her I want the best. Would it be too much trouble to show me what other, and perhaps better, dolls you may have?'

Her eyes wavered for a moment. I had the thought that she was listening to some sound I could not hear.

Abruptly her manner lost its indifference, became gracious. And at that exact moment I felt other eyes upon me, studying me, searching me. So strong was the impression that, involuntarily, I turned and peered about the shop. There was no one except the girl and me. A door was at the counter's end, but it was tightly closed. I shot a glance at the window to see whether McCann was staring in. No one was there.

Then, like the clicking of a camera shutter, the unseen gaze was gone. I turned back to the girl. She had spread a half-dozen boxes on the counter and was opening them. She looked up at me, candidly – almost sweetly. She said:

'Why, of course you may see all that we have. I am sorry if you thought me indifferent to your desires. My aunt, who makes the dolls, loves children. She would not willingly allow one who also loves them to go from here disappointed.'

It was a curious little speech, oddly stilted, enunciated half as though she were reciting from dictation. Yet it was not that which aroused my interest so much as the subtle change that had taken place in the girl herself. Her voice was no longer languid. It held a vital vibrancy. Nor was she the lifeless, listless person she had been. She was animated, even a touch of vivaciousness about her; color had crept into her face and all vagueness gone from her eyes; in them was a sparkle, faintly mocking, more than faintly malicious.

I examined the dolls.

'They are lovely,' I said at last. 'But are these the best you have? Frankly, this is rather an especial occasion – my granddaughter's seventh birthday. The price doesn't really matter as long, of course, as it is in reason—'

I heard her sigh. I looked at her. The pale eyes held their olden fear-touched stare, all sparkling mockery gone. The color had fled her face. And again, abruptly, I felt the unseen gaze upon me, more powerfully than ever before. And again I felt it shuttered off.

The door beside the counter opened.

Prepared though I had been for the extraordinary by Walters' description of the doll-maker, her appearance gave me a distinct shock. Her height, her massiveness, was amplified by the proximity of the dolls and the slender figure of the girl. It was a giantess who regarded me from the doorway – a giantess whose heavy face with its broad, high cheek bones, mustached upper lip and thick mouth produced a suggestion of masculinity grotesquely in contrast with the immense bosom.

I looked into her eyes and forgot all grotesqueness of face and figure. The eyes were enormous, a luminous black, clear, disconcertingly alive. As though they were twin spirits of life, and independent of the body. And from them poured a flood of vitality that sent along my nerves a warm tingle in which there was nothing sinister – or was not then.

With difficulty I forced my own eyes from hers. I looked for her hands. She was swathed all in black, and her hands were hidden in the folds of her ample dress. My gaze went back to her eyes, and within them was a sparkle of the mocking contempt I had seen in those of the girl. She spoke, and I knew that the vital vibrancy I had heard in the girl's voice had been an echo of those sonorously sweet, deep tones.

'What my niece has shown does not please you?'

I gathered my wits. I said: 'They are all beautiful, Madame – Madame—'

'Mandilip,' she said, serenely. 'Madame Mandilip. You do not know the name, eh?'

'It is my ill fortune,' I answered, ambiguously. 'I have a grandchild – a little girl. I want something peculiarly fine for her seventh birthday. All that I have been shown are beautiful – but I was wondering whether there was not something—'

'Something – peculiarly—' her voice lingered on the word – 'more beautiful. Well, perhaps there is. But when I favor customers peculiarly—' I now was sure she emphasized the word – 'I must know with whom I am dealing. You think me a strange shopkeeper, do you not?'

She laughed, and I marveled at the freshness, the youthfulness, the curious tingling sweetness of that laughter.

It was by a distinct effort that I brought myself back to reality, put myself again on guard. I drew a card from my case. I did not wish her to recognize me, as she would have had I given her my own card. Nor did I desire to direct her attention to anyone she could harm. I had, therefore, prepared myself by carrying the card of a doctor friend long dead. She glanced at it.

'Ah,' she said. 'You are a professional – a physician. Well, now that we know each other, come with me and I will show you of my best.'

She led me through the door and into a wide, dim corridor. She touched my arm and again I felt that strange, vital tingling. She paused at another door, and faced me.

'It is here,' she said, 'that I keep my best. My – *peculiarly* – best!'

Once more she laughed, then flung the door open.

I crossed the threshold and paused, looking about the room with swift disquietude. For here was no spacious chamber of enchantment such as Walters had described. True enough, it was somewhat larger than one would have expected. But where were the exquisite old panelings, the ancient tapestries, that magic mirror which was like a great 'half-globe of purest water,' and all those other things that had made it seem to her a Paradise?

The light came through the half-drawn curtains of a window opening upon a small, enclosed and barren yard. The walls and ceiling were of plain, stained wood. One end was entirely taken up by small, built-in cabinets with wooden doors. There was a mirror on the wall, and it was round – but there any similarity to Walters' description ended.

There was a fireplace, the kind one can find in any ordinary old New York house. On the walls were a few prints. The great table, the 'baronial board', was an entirely commonplace one, littered with dolls' clothing in various stages of completion.

My disquietude grew. If Walters had been romancing about this room, then what else in her diary was invention – or, at least, as I had surmised when I had read it, the product of a too active imagination?

Yet – she had not been romancing about the doll-maker's eyes, nor her voice; and she had not exagerated the doll-maker's appearance nor the peculiarities of the niece. The woman spoke, recalling me to myself, breaking my thoughts.

'My room interests you?'

She spoke softly, and with, I thought, a certain secret amusement.

I said: 'Any room where any true artist creates is of interest. And you are a true artist. Madame Mandilip.'

'Now, how do you know that?' she mused.

It had been a slip. I said, quickly:

'I am a lover of art. I have seen a few of your dolls. It does not take a gallery of his pictures to make one realize that Raphael, for example, was a master. One picture is enough.

She smiled, in the friendliest fashion. She closed the door behind me, and pointed to a chair beside the table.

You will not mind waiting a few minutes before I show you my dolls? There is a dress I must finish. It is promised, and soon the little one to whom I have promised it will come. It will not take me long.'

'Why, no,' I answered, and dropped into the chair.

She said, softly: 'It is quiet here. And you seem weary. You have been working hard, eh? And you are *weary*.'

I sank back into the chair. Suddenly I realized how weary I really was. For a moment my guard relaxed and I closed my eyes. I opened them to find that the doll-maker had taken her seat at the table.

And now I saw her hands. They were long and delicate and white and I knew that they were the most beautiful I had ever beheld. Just as her eyes seemed to have life of their own, so did those hands seem living things, having a being independent of the body to which they belonged. She rested them on the table. She spoke again, caressingly.

'It is well to come now and then to a quiet place. To a place where peace is. One grows so weary – so *weary*. So tired – so very *tired*."

She picked a little dress from the table and began to sew. Long white fingers plied the needle while the other hand turned and moved the small garment. How wonderful was the motion of those long white hands . . . like a rhythm . . . like a song . . . restful!

She said, in low sweet tones:

'Ah, yes – here nothing of the outer world comes. All is peace – and rest – rest—'

I drew my eyes reluctantly from the slow dance of those hands, the weaving of those long and delicate fingers which moved so rhythmically. So restfully. The doll-maker's eyes were on me, soft and gentle . . . full of that peace of which she had been telling.

It would do no harm to relax a little, gain strength for the struggle which must come. And I was tired. I had not realized how tired! My gaze went back to her hands. Strange hands – no more belonging to that huge body than did the eyes and voice.

Perhaps they did not! Perhaps that gross body was but a cloak, a covering, of the real body to which eyes and hands and voice belonged. I thought over that, watching the slow rhythms of the hands. What could the body be like to which they belonged? As beautiful as hands and eyes and voice?

She was humming some strange air. It was a slumberous, lulling melody. It crept along my tired nerves, into my weary mind – distilling sleep . . . sleep. As the hands were weaving sleep. As the eyes were pouring sleep upon me—

Sleep!

Something within me was raging, furiously. Bidding me rouse myself! Shake of this lethargy—

By the tearing effort that brought me gasping to the surface of consciousness, I knew that I must have passed far along the path of that strange sleep. And for an instant, on the threshold of complete awakening, I saw the room as Walters had seen it.

Vast, filled with mellow light, the ancient tapestries, the panelings, the carved screens behind which hidden shapes lurked laughing – laughing at me. Upon the wall the mirror – and it *was* like a great half-globe of purest water within which the images of the carvings round its frame swayed like the reflections of verdure round a clear woodland pool!

The immense chamber seemed to waver – and it was gone.

I stood beside an overturned chair in that room to which the doll-maker had led me. And the doll-maker was beside me, close. She was regarding me with a curious puzzlement and, I thought, a shadow of chagrin. It flashed upon me that she was like one who had been unexpectedly interrupted—

Interrupted! When had she left her chair? How long had I slept? What had she done to me while I had been sleeping? What had that terrific effort of will by which I had broken from her web prevented her from completing?

I tried to speak – and could not. I stood tongue-tied, furious, humiliated. I realized that I had been trapped like the veriest tyro – I who should have been all alert, suspicious of every move. Trapped by voice and eyes and weaving hands . . . by the reiterated suggestion that I was weary . . . so weary . . . that here was peace . . . and sleep . . . sleep. . . .

What had she done to me while I slept! Why could I not move! It was as though all my energy had been dissipated in that one tremendous thrust out of her web of sleep. I stood motionless, silent, spent. Not a muscle moved at command of my will. The enfeebled hands of my will reached out to them – and fell.

The doll-maker laughed. She walked to the cabinets

on the far wall. My eyes followed her, helplessly. There was no slightest loosening of the paralysis that gripped me. She pressed a spring, and the door of a cabinet slipped down.

Within the cabinet was a child-doll. A little girl, sweet-faced and smiling. I looked at it and felt a numbness at my heart. In its small, clasped hands was one of the dagger-pins, and I knew that this was the doll which had stirred in the arms of the Gilmore baby . . . had climbed from the baby's crib . . . had danced to the bed and thrust . . .

'This is one of my *peculiarly* best!' The doll-maker's eyes were on me and filled with cruel mockery. 'A good doll! A bit careless at times, perhaps. Forgetting to bring back her school-books when she goes visiting. But so obedient! Would you like her – for your grand-daughter?'

Again she laughed – youthful, tingling, evil laughter. And suddenly I knew Ricori had been right and that this woman must be killed. I summoned all my will to leap upon her. I could not move a finger.

The long white hands groped over the next cabinet and touched its hidden spring. The numbness at my heart became the pressure of a hand of ice. Staring out at me from that cabinet was Walters—

And she was crucified!

So perfect, so – *alive* was the doll that it was like seeing the girl herself through a diminishing glass. I could not think of it as a doll, but as the girl. She was dressed in her nurse's uniform. She had no cap, and her black hair hung disheveled about her face. Her arms were out-stretched, and through each palm a small nail had been thrust, pinning the hands to the back of the cabinet. The feet were bare, resting one on the other, and through the insteps had been thrust another nail. Completing the dreadful, the blasphemous, suggestion, above her head was a small placard. I read it:

'*The Burnt Martyr.*'

The doll-maker murmured – in a voice like honey garnered from flowers in hell:

'This doll has not behaved well. She has been disobedient. I punish my dolls when they do not behave well. But I see that you are distressed. Well, she has been punished enough – for the moment.'

The long white hands crept into the cabinet, drew out the nails from hands and feet. She set the doll upright, leaning against the back. She turned to me.

'You would like her for your granddaughter, perhaps? Alas! She is not for sale. She has lessons to learn before she goes again from me.'

Her voice changed, lost its diabolic sweetness, became charged with menace.

'Now listen to me – Dr Lowell! What – you did not think I knew you? I knew you from the first. You too need a lesson!' Her eyes blazed upon me. 'You shall have your lesson – you fool! You who pretend to heal the mind – and know nothing, *nothing* I say, of what the mind is. You, who conceive the mind as but a part of a machine of flesh and blood, nerve and bone – and know nothing of what it houses. You – who admit existence of nothing unless you can measure it in your test tubes or see it under your microscope. You – who define life as a chemical ferment, and consciousness as the product of cells. You fool! Yet you and this savage, Ricori, have dared to try to hamper me, to interfere with me, to hem me round with spies! Dared to threaten me –*Me* – possessor of the ancient wisdom beside which your science is as crackling of thorns under an empty pot! You fools! *I* know who are the dwellers in the mind – and the powers that manifest themselves through it – and those who dwell beyond it! They come at my call. And you think to pit your paltry knowledge against mine! You fool! Have you understood me? Speak!'

She pointed a finger at me. I felt my throat relax, knew I could speak once more.

'You hell hag!' I croaked. 'You damned murderess! You'll go to the electric chair before I'm through with you!'

She came toward me, laughing.

'You would give me to the law? But who would believe you? None! The ignorance that your science has fostered is my shield. The darkness of your unbelief is my impregnable fortress. Go play with your machines, fool! Play with your machines! But meddle with me no more!'

Her voice grew quiet, deadly.

'Now this I tell you. If you would live, if you would have live those who are dear to you – take your spies away. Ricori you cannot save. He is mine. But you – think never of me again. Pry no more into my affairs. I do not fear your spies – but they offend me. Take them away. At once. If by nightfall they are still on watch—'

She caught me by the shoulder with a grip that bruised. She pushed me toward the door.

'Go!'

I fought to muster my will, to raise my arms. Could I have done so I would have struck her down as I would a ravening beast. I could not move them. Like an automaton I walked across the room to the door. The dollmaker opened it.

There was an odd rustling noise from the cabinets. Stiffly, I turned my head.

The doll of Walters had fallen forward. It lay half over the edge. Its arms swung, as though imploring me to take it away. I could see in its palms the marks of the crucifying nails. Its eyes were fixed on mine—

'Go!' said the doll-maker. 'And remember!'

With the same stiff motion I walked through the corridor and into the shop. The girl watched me, with vague, fear-filled eyes. As though a hand were behind me, pressing me inexorably on, I passed through the shop and out of its door into the street.

I seemed to hear, did hear, the mocking evil-sweet laughter of the doll-maker!

CHAPTER FOURTEEN

The Doll-Maker Strikes

The moment I was out in the street, volition, power of movement, returned to me. In an abrupt rush of rage, I turned to re-enter the shop. A foot from it, I was brought up as against an invisible wall. I could not advance a step, could not even raise my hands to touch the door. It was as though at that point my will refused to function, or rather that my legs and arms refused to obey my will. I realized what it was – post hypnotic suggestion of an extraordinary kind, part of the same phenomena which had held me motionless before the doll-maker, and had sent me like a robot out of her lair. I saw McCann coming toward me, and for an instant had the mad idea of ordering him to enter and end Madame Mandilip with a bullet. Common sense swiftly told me that we could give no rational reason for such killing, and that we would probably expiate it within the same apparatus of execution with which I had threatened her.

McCann said: 'I was getting worried, Doc. Just about to break in on you.'

I said: 'Come on, McCann. I want to get home as quickly as possible.'

He looked at my face, and whistled.

'You look like you been through a battle, Doc.'

I answered: 'I have. And the honors are all with Madame Mandilip – so far.'

'You came out quiet enough. Not like the boss, with

the hag spitting hell in your face. What happened?'

'I'll tell you later. Just let me be quiet for awhile. I want to think.

What I actually wanted was to get back my self-possession. My mind seemed half-blind, groping for the tangible. It was as if it had been enmeshed in cobwebs of a peculiarly unpleasant character, and although I had torn loose, fragments of the web were still clinging to it. We got into the car and rolled on for some minutes in silence. Then McCann's curiosity got the better of him.

'Anyway,' he asked, 'what did you think of her?'

By this time I had come to a determination. Never had I felt anything to approach the loathing, the cold hatred, the implacable urge to kill, which this woman had aroused in me. It was not that my pride had suffered, although that was sore enough. No, it was the conviction that in the room behind the doll-shop dwelt blackest evil. Evil as inhuman and alien as though the doll-maker had in truth come straight from that hell in which Ricori believed. There could be no compromise with that evil. Nor with the woman in whom it was centered.

I said: 'McCann, in all the world there is nothing as evil as that woman. Do not let the girl slip through your fingers again. Do you think she knew last night that she had been seen?'

'I don't know. I don't think so.'

'Increase the guards in front and back of the place at once. Do it openly, so that the women cannot help noticing it. They will think, unless the girl is aware that she was observed, that we are still in ignorance of the other exit. They will think we believe she managed to slip out unseen either at front or back. Have a car in readiness at each end of the street where she keeps the coupé. Be careful not to arouse their suspicions. If the girl appears, follow her—' I hesitated.

McCann asked: 'And then what?'

'I want her taken – abducted, kidnaped – whatever you choose to call it. It must be done with the utmost quietness. I leave that to you. You know how such things are done better than I. Do it quickly and do it quietly. But not too near the doll-shop – as far away from it as you can. Gag the girl, tie her up if necessary. But get her. Then search the car thoroughly. Bring the girl to me at my house – with whatever you find. Do you understand?'

He said: 'If she shows, we'll get her. You going to put her through the third degree?'

'That – and something more. I want to see what the doll-maker will do. It may goad her into some action which will enable us to lay hands on her legitimately. Bring her within reach of the law. She may or may not have other and invisible servants, but my intention is to deprive her of the visible one. It may make the others visible. At the least, it will cripple her.'

He looked at me, curiously: She musta hit you pretty hard, Doc.'

'She did,' I answered curtly. He hesitated.

'You going to tell the boss about this?' he asked at last.

'I may or I may not – to-night. It depends upon his condition. Why?'

'Well, if we're going to pull off anything like a kidnaping, I think he ought to know.'

I said, sharply: 'McCann, I told you Ricori's message was that you were to obey orders from me as though they were from him. I have given you your orders. I accept all the responsibility.'

157

'Okay,' he answered, but I could see that his doubt still lingered.

Now, assuming Ricori had sufficiently recovered, there was no real reason why I should not tell him what had happened during my encounter with Madame Mandilip. It was different with Braile. More than suspecting, as I did, the attachment between him and Walters, I could not tell him of the crucified doll – and even now I thought of it not as a doll crucified, but as Walters crucified. If I told him, I knew well that there would be no holding him back from instant attack upon the doll-maker. I did not want that.

But I was aware of a most stubborn reluctance to tell Ricori the details of my visit. The same held good for Braile in other matters beside the Walters doll. And why did I feel the same way about McCann? I set it down to wounded vanity.

We stopped in front of my house. It was then close to six. Before getting out of the car I repeated my instructions. McCann nodded.

'Okay, Doc. If she comes out, we get her.'

I went into the house, and found a note from Braile saying that he would not be in to see me until after dinner. I was glad of that. I dreaded the ordeal of his questions. I learned that Ricori was asleep, and that he had been regaining strength with astonishing rapidity. I instructed the nurse to tell him, should he awaken, that I would visit him after I had dined. I lay down, endeavoring to snatch a little sleep before eating.

I could not sleep – constantly the face of the doll-maker came before me whenever I began to relax into a doze, throwing me into intense wakefulness.

At seven I arose and ate a full and excellent dinner, deliberately drinking at least twice the amount of wine

I ordinarily permit myself, finishing with strong coffee. When I arose from the table I felt distinctly better, mentally alert and master of myself once more – or so I believed. I had decided to apprise Ricori of my instructions to McCann concerning the abduction of the girl. I realized that this was certain to bring down upon me a minute catechism concerning my visit to the doll-shop, but I had formulated the story I intended to tell—

It was with a distinct shock that I realized that this story was all that I *could* tell! Realized that I could not communicate to the others the portions I had deleted, even if I desired. And that this was by command of the doll-maker – post hypnotic suggestion which was a part of those other inhibitions she had laid upon my will; those same inhibitions which had held me powerless before her, had marched me out of her shop like a robot and thrust me back from her door, when I would have re-entered!

During that brief tranced sleep she had said to me: 'This and this you must not tell. This and this you may.'

I should not speak of the child-doll with the angelic face and the dagger-pin which had pricked the bubble of Gilmore's life. I could not speak of the Walters doll and its crucifixion. I could not speak of the doll-maker's tacit admission that she had been responsible for the deaths that had first led us to her.

However, this realization made me feel even better. Here at last was something understandable – the tangibility for which I had been groping; something that had in it nothing of sorcery – nor of dark power; something entirely in the realm of my own science. I had done the same thing to patients, many times, bringing their minds

159

back to normality by these same post-hypnotic suggestions.

Also, there was a way by which I could wash my own mind clean of the doll-maker's suggestions, if I chose. Should I do this? Stubbornly, I decided I would not. It would be an admission that I was afraid of Madame Mandilip. I hated her, yes – but I did not fear her. Knowing now her technique, it would be folly not to observe its results with myself as the laboratory experiment. I told myself that I had run the gamut of those suggestions – that whatever else it had been her intention to implant within my mind had been held back by my unexpected awakening—

Ah, but the doll-maker had spoken the truth when she called me—fool!

When Braile appeared, I was able to meet him calmly. Hardly had I greeted him when Ricori's nurse called up to say her patient was wide-awake and anxious to see me.

I said to Braile: 'This is fortunate. Come along. It will save me from telling the same story twice over.'

He asked: 'What story?'

'My interview with Madame Mandilip.'

He said, incredulously: 'You've seen her!'

'I spent the afternoon with her. She is most – interesting. Come and hear about it.'

I led the way rapidly to the Annex, deaf to his questions. Ricori was sitting up. I made a brief examination. Although still somewhat weak, he could be discharged as a patient. I congratulated him on what was truly a remarkable recovery. I whispered to him:

'I've seen your witch – and talked to her. I have much to tell you. Bid your guards take their stations outside the door. I will dismiss the nurse for a time.'

When guards and nurse were gone, I launched into an account of the day's happenings, beginning with my summons to the Gilmore apartment by McCann. Ricori listened, face grim, as I repeated Mollie's story. He said:

'Her brother – and now her husband! Poor, poor Mollie! But she shall be avenged! *Si!* – greatly so! Yes!'

I gave my grossly incomplete version of my encounter with Madame Mandilip. I told Ricori what I had bidden McCann to do. I said:

'And so to-night, at least, we can sleep in peace. For if the girl comes out with the dolls, McCann gets her. If she does not, then nothing can happen. I am quite certain that without her the doll-maker cannot strike. I hope you approve, Ricori.'

He studied me for a moment, intently.

'I do approve, Dr. Lowell. Most greatly do I approve. You have done as I would have done. But – I do not think you have told us all that happened between you and the witch.

'Nor do I,' said Braile.

I arose.

'At any rate, I've told you the essentials. And I'm dead tired. I'm going to take a bath and go to bed. It's now nine-thirty. If the girl does come out it won't be before eleven, probably later. I'm going to sleep until McCann fetches her. If he doesn't, I'm going to sleep all night. That's final. Save your questions for the morning.'

Ricori's searching gaze had never left me. He said:

'Why not sleep here? Would it not be safer – for you?'

I succumbed to a wave of intense irritation. My pride

had been hurt enough by my behaviour with the doll-maker and the manner she had outwitted me. And the suggestion that I hide from her behind the guns of his men opened the wound afresh.

'I am no child,' I answered angrily. 'I am quite able to take care of myself. I do not have to live behind a screen of gunmen—'

I stopped, sorry that I had said that. But Ricori betrayed no anger. He nodded, and dropped back on his pillows.

'You have told me what I wanted to know. You fared very badly with the witch, Dr. Lowell. And you have not told us all the – essentials.'

I said: 'I am sorry, Ricori!'

'Don't be.' For the first time he smiled. 'I understand, perfectly. I also am somewhat of a psychologist. But I say this to you – it matters little whether McCann does or does not bring the girl to us tonight. Tomorrow the witch dies – and the girl with her.'

I made no answer. I recalled the nurse, and re-stationed the guards within the room. Whatever confidence I might feel, I was taking no chances with Ricori's safety. I had not told him of the doll-maker's direct threat against him, but I had not forgotten it.

Braile accompanied me to my study. He said, apologetically:

'I know you must be damned tired, Lowell, and I don't want to pester you. But will you let me stay in your room with you while you are sleeping?'

I said with the same stubborn irritability:

'For God's sake, Braile, didn't you hear what I told Ricori? I'm much obliged and all of that, but it applies to you as well.'

He said quietly: 'I am going to stay right here in the

162

study, wide-awake, until McCann comes or dawn comes. If I hear any sounds in your room, I'm coming in. Whenever I want to take a look at you to see whether you are all right, I'm coming in. Don't lock your door, because if you do I'll break it down. Is that all quite clear?'

I grew angrier still. He said:

'I mean it.'

I said: 'All right. Do as you damned please.'

I went into my bedroom, slamming the door behind me. But I did not lock it.

I was tired, there was no doubt about that. Even an hour's sleep would be something. I decided not to bother with the bath, and began to undress. I was removing my shirt when I noticed a tiny pin upon its left side over my heart. I opened the shirt and looked at the under side. Fastened there was one of the knotted cords!

I took a step toward the door, mouth open to call Braile. Then I stopped short. I would not show it to Braile. That would mean endless questioning. And I wanted to sleep.

God! But I wanted to sleep.

Better to burn the cord. I searched for a match to touch fire to it – I heard Braile's step at the door and thrust it hastily in my trousers' pocket.

'What do you want?' I called.

'Just want to see you get into bed all right.'

He opened the door a trifle. What he wanted to discover, of course, was whether I had locked it. I said nothing, and went on undressing.

My bedroom is a large, high-ceilinged room on the second floor of my home. It is at the back of the house adjoining my study. There are two windows which look out on the little garden. They are framed by the creeper. The room has a chandelier, a massive, old-fashioned thing covered with prisms – lusters I think they are called, long pendants of cut-glass in six circles from which rise the candle-holders. It is a small replica of one of the lovely Colonial chandeliers in Independence Hall at Philadelphia, and when I bought the house I would not allow it to be taken down, nor even be wired for electric bulbs. My bed is at the end of the room, and when I turn upon my left side I can see the windows outlined by faint reflections. The same reflections are caught by the prisms so that the chandelier becomes a nebulously glimmering tiny cloud. It is restful, sleep-inducing. There is an ancient pear tree in the garden, the last survivor of an orchard which in spring, in New York's halcyon days, lifted to the sun its flowered arms. The chandelier is just beyond the foot of the bed. The switch which controls my lights is at the head of my bed. At the side of the room is an old fireplace, its sides of carved marble and with a wide mantel at the top. To vizualize fully what follows, it is necessary to keep this arrangement in mind.

By the time I had undressed, Braile, evidently assured of my docility, had closed the door and gone back into the study. I took the knotted cord, the witch's ladder, and threw it contemptuously on the table. I suppose there was something of bravado in the action; perhaps, if I had not felt so sure of McCann, I would have pursued my original intention of burning it. I mixed myself a sedative, turned off the lights and lay down to sleep. The sedative took quick effect.

I sank deep and deeper into a sea of sleep . . . deeper . . . and deeper . . .

I awoke.

164

I looked around me . . . how had I come to this strange place? I was standing within a shallow circular pit, grass lined. The rim of the pit came only to my knees. The pit was in the center of a circular, level meadow, perhaps a quarter of a mile in diameter. This, too, was covered with grass; strange grass, purple flowered. Around the grassy circle drooped unfamiliar trees . . . trees scaled with emeralds green and scarlet . . . trees with pendulous branches covered with fernlike leaves and threaded with slender vines that were like serpents. The trees circled the meadow, watchful, alert . . . watching me . . . waiting for me to move. . . .

No, it was not the trees that were watching! There were things hidden among the trees, lurking . . . malignant things . . . evil things . . . and it was they who were watching me, waiting for me to move!

But how had I gotten here? I looked down at my legs, stretched my arms . . . I was clad in the blue pajamas in which I had gone to bed . . . gone to my bed in my New York house . . . in my house in New York . . . how had I come here? I did not seem to be dreaming. . . .

Now I saw that three paths led out of the shallow pit. They passed over the edge, and stretched, each in a different direction, toward the woods. And suddenly I knew that I must take one of these paths, and that it was vitally important that I pick the right one . . . that only one could be traversed safely . . . that the other two would lead me into the power of those lurking things.

The pit began to contract. I felt its bottom lifting beneath my feet. The pit was thrusting me out! I leaped upon the path at my right, and began to walk slowly along it. Then involuntarily I began to run, faster and faster along it, toward the woods. As I drew nearer I saw that the path pierced the woods straight as an arrow flight, and that it was about three feet wide and bordered closely by the trees, and that it vanished in the dim green distance. Faster and faster I ran. Now I had entered the woods, and the unseen things were gathering among the trees that bordered the path, thronging the borders, rushing silently from all the wood. What those things were, what they would do to me if they caught me I did not know. . . . I only knew that nothing that I could imagine of agony could equal what I would experience if they did catch me.

On and on I raced through the wood, each step a nightmare. I felt hands stretching out to clutch me . . . heard shrill whisperings. . . . Sweating, trembling, I broke out of the wood and raced over a vast plain that stretched, treeless, to the distant horizon. The plain was trackless, pathless, and covered with brown and withered grass. It was like, it came to me, the blasted heath of Macbeth's three witches. No matter . . . it was better than the haunted wood. I paused and looked back at the trees. I felt from them the gaze of myriads of the evil eyes.

I turned my back, and began to walk over the withered plain. I looked up at the sky. The sky was misty green. High up in it two cloudy orbs began to glow . . . black suns . . . no, they were not suns . . . they were eyes. . . .

The eyes of the doll-maker!

They stared down at me from the misty green sky . . .

Over the horizon of that strange world two gigantic hands began to lift . . . began to creep toward me . . . to catch me and hurl me back into the wood . . . white hands with long fingers . . . and each of the long white fingers a living thing. . . .

The hands of the doll-maker!

Closer came the eyes, and closer writhed the hands. From the sky came peal upon peal of laughter . . . The laughter of the doll-maker!

That laughter still ringing in my ears, I awakened – or seemed to awaken. I was in my room sitting bolt upright in my bed. I was dripping with sweat, and my heart was pumping with a pulse that shook my body. I could see the chandelier glimmering in the light from the windows like a small nebulous cloud. I could see the windows faintly outlined . . . it was very still . . .

There was a movement at one of the windows. I would get up from the bed and see what it was—

I could not move!

A faint greenish glow began within the room. At first it was like the flickering phosphorescence one sees upon a decaying log. It waxed and waned, waxed and waned, but grew ever stronger. My room became plain. The chandelier gleamed like a decaying emerald—

There was a little face at the window! A doll's face! My heart leaped, then curdled with despair. I thought: 'McCann has failed! It is the end!'

The doll looked at me, grinning. Its face was smooth shaven, that of a man about forty. The nose was long, the mouth wide and thin-lipped. The eyes were close-set under bushy brows. They glittered, red as rubies.

The doll crept over the sill. It slid, head-first, into the room. It stood for a moment on its head, legs waving. It somersaulted twice. It came to its feet, one little hand at its lips, red eyes upon mine – waiting. As though expecting applause! It was dressed in the tights and jacket of a circus acrobat. It bowed to me. Then with a flourish, it pointed to the window.

Another little face was peering there. It was austere,

cold, the face of a man of sixty. It had small side whiskers. It stared at me with the expression I supposed a banker might wear when someone he hates applies to him for a loan – I found the thought oddly amusing. Then abruptly I ceased to feel amused.

A banker-doll! An acrobat-doll!

The dolls of two of those who had suffered the unknown death!

The banker-doll stepped with dignity down from the window. It was in full evening dress, swallow-tails, stiff shirt – all perfect. It turned and with the same dignity raised a hand to the window sill. Another doll stood there – the doll of a woman about the same age as the banker-doll, and garbed like it in correct evening dress.

The spinster!

Mincingly, the spinster-doll took the proffered hand. She jumped lightly to the floor.

Through the window came a fourth doll, all in spangled tights from neck to feet. It took a flying leap, landing beside the acrobat-doll. It looked up at me with grinning face, then bowed.

The four dolls began to march toward me, the acrobats leading, and behind them with slow and stately step, the spinster-doll and banker-doll – arm in arm.

Grotesque, fantastic, these they were – but not humorous. God – no! Or if there were anything of humor about them, it was that at which only devils laugh.

I thought, desperately: 'Braile is just on the other side of the door! If I could only make some sound!'

The four dolls halted and seemed to consult. The acrobats pirouetted, and reached to their backs. They drew from the hidden sheaths their dagger-pins. In the hands of banker-doll and spinster-doll appeared similar

168

weapons. They presented the points toward me, like swords.

The four resumed their march to my bed . . .

The red eyes of the second acrobat-doll – the trapeze performer, I knew him now to be – had rested on the chandelier. He paused, studying it. He pointed to it, thrust the dagger-pin back into its sheath, and bent his knees, hands cupped in front of them. The first doll nodded, then stood, plainly measuring the height of the chandelier from the floor and considering the best approach to it. The second doll pointed to the mantel, and the pair of them swarmed up its sides to the broad ledge. The elderly pair watched them, seemingly much interested. They did not sheath their dagger-pins.

The acrobat-doll bent, and the trapeze-doll put a little foot in its cupped hands. The first doll straightened, and the second flew across the gap between mantel and chandelier, caught one of the prismed circles, and swung. Immediately the other doll leaped outward, caught the chandelier and swung beside its spangled mate.

I saw the heavy old fixture tremble and sway. Down upon the floor came crashing a dozen of the prisms. In the dead stillness, it was like an explosion.

I heard Braile running to the door. He threw it open. He stood on the threshold. I could see him plainly in the green glow, but I knew that he could not see – that to him the room was in darkness. He cried:

'Lowell! Are you all right? Turn on the lights!'

I tried to call out. To warn him. Useless!

He groped forward, around the foot of the bed, to the switch. I think that then he saw the dolls. He stopped short, directly beneath the chandelier, looking up.

And as he did so the doll above him swung by one hand, drew its dagger-pin from its sheath and dropped upon Braile's shoulders, stabbing viciously at his throat!

Braile shrieked – once. The shriek changed into a dreadful bubbling sigh. . . .

And then I saw the chandelier sway and lurch. It broke from its ancient fastenings. It fell with a crash that shook the house, down upon Braile and the doll-devil ripping at his throat.

Abruptly the green glow disappeared. There was a scurrying in the room like the running of great rats.

The paralysis dropped from me. I threw my hand round to the switch and turned on the lights; leaped from the bed.

Little figures were scrambling up and out of the window. There were four muffled reports like pop-guns. I saw Ricori at the door, on each side of him a guard with silenced automatic, shooting at the window.

I bent over Braile. He was quite dead. The falling chandelier had dropped upon his head, crushing the skull. But—

Braile had been dying before the chandelier had fallen . . . his throat ripped . . . the carotid artery severed.

The doll that had murdered him – was gone!

CHAPTER FIFTEEN

The Witch Girl

I stood up. I said bitterly:

'You were right, Ricori – her servants are better than yours.'

He did not answer, looking down at Braile with pity-filled face.

I said: 'If all your men fulfil their promises like McCann, that you are still alive I count as one of the major miracles.'

'As for McCann,' he turned his gaze to me somberly, 'he is both intelligent and loyal. I will not condemn him unheard. And I say to you, Dr. Lowell, that if you had shown more frankness to me this night – Dr. Braile would not be dead.'

I winced at that – there was too much truth in it. I was racked by regret and grief and helpless rage. If I had not let my cursed pride control me, if I had told them all that I could of my encounter with the doll-maker, explained why there were details I was unable to tell, given myself over to Braile for a cleansing counter-hypnotization – no, if I had but accepted Ricori's offer of protection, or Braile's to watch over me while asleep – then this could not have happened.

I looked into the study and saw there Ricori's nurse. I could hear whispering outside the study doors – servants, and others from the Annex who had been attracted by the noise of the falling chandelier. I said to the nurse, quite calmly:

'The chandelier fell while Dr. Braile was standing at the foot of my bed talking to me. It has killed him. But do not tell the others that. Only say that the chandelier fell, injuring Dr. Braile. Send them back to their beds – say that we are taking Dr. Braile to the hospital. Then return with Porter and clean up what you can of the blood. Leave the chandelier as it is.'

When she had gone I turned to Ricori's gunmen.

'What did you see when you shot?'

One answered: 'They looked like monkeys to me.'

The other said: 'Or midgets.'

I looked at Ricori, and read in his face what he had seen. I stripped the light blanket from the bed.

'Ricori,' I said. 'let your men lift Braile and wrap him in this. Then have them carry him into the small room next to the study and place him on the cot.'

He nodded to them, and they lifted Braile from the débris of shattered glass and bent metal. His face and neck had been cut by the broken prisms and by some chance one of these wounds was close to the spot where the dagger-pin of the doll had been thrust. It was deep, and had probably caused a second severance of the carotid artery. I followed with Ricori into the small room. They placed the body on the cot and Ricori ordered them to go back to the bedroom and watch while the nurses were there. He closed the door of the small room behind them, then turned to me.

'What are you going to do, Dr. Lowell?'

What I felt like doing was weeping, but I answered: 'It is a coroner's case, of course. I must notify the police at once.'

'What are you going to tell them?'

'What did you see at the window, Ricori?'

'I saw – the dolls!'

172

'And I. Can I tell the police what did kill Braile – before the chandelier fell? You know I cannot. No, I shall tell them that we were talking when, without warning, the fixture dropped upon him. Splintered glass from the pendants pierced his throat. What else can I say? And they will believe that readily enough when they would not believe the truth—'

I hesitated, then my reserve broke; for the first time in many years, I wept.

'Ricori – you were right. Not McCann but I am to blame for this – the vanity of an old man – had I spoken freely, fully – he would be alive . . . but I did not . . . I did not . . . I am his murderer. . . .'

He comforted me – gently as a woman. . . .'

'It was not your fault. You could not have done otherwise . . . being what you are . . . thinking as you have so long thought. If in your unbelief, your entirely natural unbelief, the witch found her opportunity . . . still, it was not your fault. But now she shall find no more opportunities. Her cup is full and overflowing. . . .'

He put his hands on my shoulders.

'Do not notify the police for a time – not until we hear from McCann. It is now close to twelve and he will telephone even if he does not come. I will go to my room and dress. For when I have heard from Mc-Cann – I must leave you.'

'What do you mean to do, Ricori?'

'Kill the witch,' he answered quietly. 'Kill her and the girl. Before the day comes. I have waited too long. I will wait no longer. She shall kill no more.'

I felt a wave of weakness. I dropped into a chair. My sight dimmed. Ricori gave me water, and I drank thirstily. Through the roaring in my ears I heard a knocking at the door and the voice of one of Ricori's men:

'McCann is here.'

Ricori said: 'Tell him to come in.'

The door opened. McCann strode into the room.

'I got her—'

He stopped short, staring at us. His eyes fell upon the covered body upon the cot and his face grew grim:

'What's happened?'

Ricori answered: 'The dolls killed Dr. Braile.

You captured the girl too late, McCann. Why?'

'Killed Braile? The dolls! God!' McCann's voice was as though a hand had gripped his throat.

Ricori asked: 'Where is the girl, McCann?'

He answered, dully: 'Down in the car, gagged and tied.'

Ricori asked: '*When* did you get her? And *where*?'

Looking at McCann, I suddenly felt a great pity and sympathy for him. It sprang from my own remorse and shame. I said:

'Sit down, McCann. I am far more to blame for what has happened than you can possibly be.'

Ricori said, coldly: 'Leave me to be judge of that. McCann, did you place cars at each end of the street, as Dr. Lowell instructed?'

'Yes.'

'Then begin your story at that point.'

McCann said: 'She comes into the street. It's close to eleven. I'm at the east end an' Paul at the west. I say to Tony: 'We got the wench pocketed!' She carries two suitcases. She looks around an' trots where we located her car. She opens the door. When she comes out she rides west where Paul is. I've told Paul what the Doc tells me, not to grab her too close to the doll-

174

shop. I see Paul tail her. I shoot down the street an'
tail Paul.

The coupé turn into West Broadway. There she gets
the break, a Staten Island boat is just in an' the street's
lousy with a herd of cars. A Ford shoots over to the
left, trying to pass another. Paul hits the Ford and
wraps himself round one of the El's pillars. There's a
mess. I'm a minute or two getting out the jam. When
I do, the coupé's outa sight.

'I hop down an' telephone Rod. I tell him to get the
wench when she shows up, even if they have to rope
her off the steps of the doll-shop. An' when they get
her, bring her right here.

'I come up here. I figure maybe she's headed this
way. I coast along by here an' then take a look in the
Park, I figure the doll-hag's been getting all the breaks
an' now one's due me. I get it. I see the coupé parked
under some trees. We get the gal. She don't put up no
fight at all. But we gag her an' put her in the car. Tony
rolls the coupé away an' searches it. There ain't a thing
in it but the two suitcases an' they're empty. We bring
the gal here.'

I asked: 'How long between when you caught the
girl and your arrival?'

'Ten – fifteen minutes, maybe. Tony nigh took the
coupé to pieces. An' that took time.'

I looked at Ricori. McCann must have come upon
the girl just about the moment Braile had died. He
nodded:

'She was waiting for the dolls, of course.'

McCann asked: 'What do you want me to do with
her?'

He looked at Ricori, not at me. Ricori said nothing,
staring at McCann with a curious intentness. But I saw

175

`him clench his left hand, then open it fingers wide. McCann said:

'Okay, boss.'

He started toward the door. It did not take unusual acumen to know that he had been given orders, nor could their significance be mistaken.

'Stop!' I intercepted him and stood with my back against the door. 'Listen to me, Ricori. I have something to say about this. Dr. Braile was as close to me as Peters to you. Whatever the guilt of Madame Mandilip, this girl is helpless to do other than what she orders her. Her will is absolutely controlled by the doll-maker. I strongly suspect that a good part of the time she is under complete hypnotic control. I cannot forget that she tried to save Walters. I will not see her murdered.'

Ricori said: 'If you are right, all the more reason she should be destroyed quickly. Then the witch cannot make use of her before she herself is destroyed.'

'I will not have it, Ricori. And there is another reason. I want to question her. I may discover how Madame Mandilip does these things – the mystery of the dolls – the ingredients of the salve – whether there are others who share her knowledge. All this and more, the girl may know. And if she does know, I can make her tell.'

McCann said cynically: 'Yeah?'

Ricori asked: 'How?'

I answered grimly: 'By using the same trap in which the doll-maker caught me.'

For a full minute Ricori considered me, gravely.

'Dr. Lowell,' he said, 'for the last time I yield my judgment to yours in this matter. I think you are wrong. I know that I was wrong when I did not kill the witch that day I met her. I believe that every moment this

176

girl is permitted to remain alive is a moment laden with danger for us all. Nevertheless, I yield – for the last time.'

'McCann,' I said, 'bring the girl into my office. Wait until I get rid of anyone who may be downstairs.'

I went downstairs, McCann and Ricori following. No one was there. I placed on my desk a development of the Luys mirror, a device used first at the Salpêtrière in Paris to induce hypnotic sleep. It consists of two parallel rows of small reflectors revolving in opposite directions. A ray of light plays upon them in such a manner as to cause their surfaces alternately to gleam and darken. A most useful device, and one to which I believed the girl, long sensitized to hypnotic suggestion, must speedily succumb. I placed a comfortable chair at the proper angle, and subdued the lights so that they could not compete with the hypnotic mirror.

I had hardly completed these arrangements when McCann and another of Ricori's henchmen brought in the girl. They placed her in the easy chair, and I took from her lips the cloth with which she had been silenced.

Ricori said: 'Tony, go out to the car. McCann, you stay here.'

CHAPTER SIXTEEN

End of the Witch Girl

The girl made no resistance whatever. She seemed entirely withdrawn into herself, looking up at me with the same vague stare I had noted on my visit to the doll-shop. I took her hands. She let them rest passively in mine. They were very cold. I said to her, gently, reassuringly:

'My child, no one is going to hurt you. Rest and relax. Sink back in the chair. I only want to help you. Sleep if you wish. Sleep.'

She did not seem to hear, still regarding me with that vague gaze. I released her hands. I took my own chair, facing her, and set the little mirrors revolving. Her eyes turned to them at once, rested upon them, fascinated. I watched her body relax; she sank back in her chair. Her eyelids began to droop—

'Sleep,' I said softly. 'Here none can harm you. While you sleep none can harm you. Sleep . . . sleep. . . .'

Her eyes closed; she sighed.

I said: 'You are asleep. You will not awaken until I bid you. You cannot awaken until I bid you.'

She repeated in a murmuring, childish voice: 'I am asleep; I cannot awaken until you bid me.'

I stopped the whirling mirrors. I said to her: 'There are some questions I am going to ask you. You will listen, and you will answer me truthfully. You cannot answer them except truthfully. You know that.'

She echoed, still in that faint childish voice: 'I must answer you truthfully. I know that.'

I could not refrain from darting a glance of triumph at Ricori and McCann. Ricori was crossing himself, staring at me with wide eyes in which were both doubt and awe. I knew he was thinking that I, too, knew witchcraft. McCann sat chewing nervously. And staring at the girl.

I began my questions, choosing at first those least likely to disturb. I asked:

'Are you truly Madame Mandilip's niece?'

'No.'

'Who are you, then?'

'I do not know.'

'When did you join her, and why?'

'Twenty years ago. I was in a *crèche*, a foundling asylum at Vienna. She took me from it. She taught me to call her my aunt. But she is not.'

'Where have you lived since then?'

'In Berlin, in Paris, then London, Prague, Warsaw.'

'Did Madame Mandilip make her dolls in each of these places?'

She did not answer; she shuddered; her eyelids began to tremble.

'Sleep! Remember, you cannot awaken until I bid you! Sleep! Answer me.'

She whispered: 'Yes.'

'And they killed in each city?'

'Yes.'

'Sleep. Be at ease. Nothing is going to harm you—'
Her disquietude had again become marked, and I veered for a moment from the subject of the dolls. 'Where was Madame Mandilip born?'

'I do not know.'

'How old is she?'

'I do not know. I have asked her, and she has laughed and said that time is nothing to her. I was five years old when she took me. She looked then just as she does now.'

Has she any accomplices – I mean are there others who make the dolls?'

'One. She taught him. He was her lover in Prague.'

'Her lover!' I exclaimed, incredulously – the image of the immense gross body, the great breasts, the heavy horselike face of the doll-maker rising before my eyes. She said:

'I know what you are thinking. But she has another body. She wears it when she pleases. It is a beautiful body. It belongs to her eyes, her hands, her voice. When she wears that body she is beautiful. She is terrifyingly beautiful. I have seen her wear it many times.'

Another body! An illusion, of course . . . like the enchanted room Walters had described . . . and which I had glimpsed when breaking from the hypnotic web in which she had enmeshed me . . . a picture drawn by the doll-maker's mind in the mind of the girl. I dismissed that, and drove to the heart of the matter.

She kills by two methods, does she not – by the salve and by the dolls?'

'Yes, by the unguent and the dolls.'

'How many has she killed by the unguent in New York?'

She answered, indirectly: 'She has made fourteen dolls since we came here.'

So there were other cases that had not been reported to me! I asked:

'And how many have the dolls killed?'

'Twenty.'

I heard Ricori curse, and shot him a warning look. He was leaning forward, white and tense; McCann had stopped his chewing.

'How does she make the dolls?'

'I do not know.'

'Do you know how she prepares the unguent?'

'No. She does that secretly.'

'What is it that activates the dolls?'

'You mean makes them – alive?'

'Yes.'

'Something from the dead!'

Again I heard Ricori cursing softly. I said: 'If you do not know how the dolls are made, you must know what is necessary to make them – alive. What is it?'

She did not answer.

'You must answer me. You must obey me. Speak!'

She said: 'Your question is not clear. I have told you that something of the dead makes them alive. What else is it you would know?'

'Begin from where one who poses for a doll first meets Madame Mandilip to the last step when the doll – as you put it – becomes alive.'

She spoke, dreamily:

'She has said one must come to her of his own will. He must consent of his own volition, without coercion, to let her make the doll. That he does not know to what he is consenting matters nothing. She must begin the first model immediately. Before she completes the second – the doll that is to live – she must find opportunity to apply the unguent. She has said of this unguent that it liberates one of those who dwell within the mind, and that this one must come to her and enter the doll. She has said that this one is not the sole tenant of the mind, but with the others she has no concern.

Nor does she select all of those who come before her. How she knows those with whom she can deal, or what there is about them which makes her select them, I do not know. She makes the second doll. At the instant of its completion he who has posed for it begins to die. When he is dead – the doll lives. It obeys her – as they all obey her . . .'

She paused, then said, musingly . . . 'All except one—'

'And that one?'

'She who was your nurse. She will not obey. My – aunt – torments her, punishes her . . . still she cannot control her. I brought the little nurse here last night with another doll to kill the man my – aunt – cursed. The nurse came, but she fought the other doll and saved the man. It is something my aunt cannot understand . . . it perplexes her . . . and it gives me . . . hope!'

Her voice trailed away. Then suddenly, with energy, she said:

'You must make haste. I should be back with the dolls. Soon she will be searching for me. I must go . . . or she will come for me . . . and then . . . if she finds me here . . . she will kill me. . . .'

I said: 'You brought the dolls to kill me?'

'Of course.'

'Where are the dolls now?'

She answered: 'They were coming back to me. Your men caught me before they could reach me. They will go . . . home. The dolls travel quickly when they must. It is more difficult without me . . . that it all . . . but they will return to her . . .'

'Why do the dolls kill?'

'To . . . please . . . her.'

I said: 'The knotted cord, what part does it play?'

She answered: 'I do not know – but she says—'
Then suddenly, desperately, like a frightened child,
she whispered: 'She is searching for me! Her eyes are
looking for me . . . her hands are groping . . . she sees
me! Hide me! Oh, hide me from her . . . quick . . .'

I said: 'Sleep more deeply! Go down – down deep –
deeper still into sleep. Now she cannot find you! Now
you are hidden from her!'

She whispered: 'I am deep in sleep. She has lost me.
I am hidden. But she is hovering over me . . . she is still
searching. . . .'

Ricori and McCann had left their chairs and were
beside me.

Ricori asked:

'You believe the witch is after her?'

'No,' I answered. 'But this is not an unexpected development. The girl has been under the woman's control so long, and so completely, that the reaction is
natural. It may be the result of suggestion, or it may
be the reasoning of her own subconsciousness . . . she
has been breaking commands . . . she has been threatened with punishment if she should—'

The girl screamed, agonized:

'She sees me! She has found me! Her hands are
reaching out to me!'

'Sleep! Sleep deeper still! She cannot hurt you.
Again she has lost you!'

The girl did not answer, but a faint moaning was
audible, deep in her throat.

McCann swore, huskily: 'Christ! Can't you help
her?'

Ricori, eyes unnaturally bright in a chalky face,
said: 'Let her die! It will save us trouble!'

I said to the girl, sternly:

'Listen to me and obey. I am going to count five. When I come to five – awaken! Awaken at once! You will come up from sleep so swiftly that she cannot catch you! Obey!'

I counted, slowly, since to have awakened her at once would, in all likelihood, have brought her to the death which her distorted mind told her was threatened by the doll-maker.

'One – two – three—'

An appalling scream came from the girl. And then—

'She's caught me! Her hands are around my heart. . . . Ah-h-h . . .'

Her body bent; a spasm ran through her. Her body relaxed and sank limply in the chair. Her eyes opened, stared blankly; her jaw dropped.

I ripped open her bodice, set my stethoscope to her heart. It was still.

And then from the dead throat issued a voice organ-toned, sweet, laden with menace and contempt . . .

'You fools!'

The voice of Madame Mandilip!

CHAPTER SEVENTEEN

Burn Witch Burn!

Curiously enough, Ricori was the least affected of the three of us. My own flesh had crept. McCann, although he had never heard the doll-maker's voice, was greatly shaken. And it was Ricori who broke the silence.

'You are sure the girl is dead?'

'There is no possible doubt of it, Ricori.'

He nodded to McCann: 'Carry her down to the car.'

I asked: 'What are you going to do?'

He answered: 'Kill the witch.' He quoted with satiric unctuousness: 'In death they shall not be divided.' He said, passionately: 'As in hell they shall burn together *forever*!'

He looked at me, sharply.

'You do not approve of this, Dr. Lowell?'

'Ricori, I don't know – I honestly do not know. To-day I would have killed her with my own hands . . . but now the rage is spent . . . what you have threatened is against all my instincts, all my habits of thought, all my convictions of how justice should be administered. It seems to me – murder!'

He said: 'You heard the girl. Twenty in this city alone killed by the dolls. And fourteen dolls. Fourteen who died as Peters did!'

'But, Ricori, no court could consider allegations under hypnosis as evidence. It may be true, it may not be. The girl was abnormal. What she told might be only her imaginings – without supporting evidence, no court on earth could accept it as a basis for action.'

He said: 'No – no *earthly* court—' He gripped my shoulders. He asked: 'Do you believe it was truth?'

I could not answer, for deep within me I felt it was truth. He said:

'Precisely, Dr. Lowell! You have answered me. You know, as I know, that he girl did speak the truth. You know, as I know, that our law cannot punish the witch. That is why I must kill her. In doing that, I, Ricori, am no murderer. No, I am God's executioner!'

He waited for me to speak. Again I could not answer.

'McCann' – he pointed to the girl – 'do as I told you. Then return.'

And when McCann had gone out with the frail body in his arms, Ricori said:

'Dr. Lowell – you must go with me to witness this execution.'

I recoiled at that. I said:

'Ricori, I can't. I am utterly weary – in body and mind. I have gone through too much to-day. I am broken with grief—'

'You must go,' he interrupted, 'if we have to carry you, gagged as the girl was, and bound. I will tell you why. You are at war with yourself. Alone, it is possible your scientific doubts might conquer, that you would attempt to halt me before I have done what I swear by Christ, His Holy Mother, and the Saints, I shall do. You might yield to weariness and place the whole matter before the police. I will not take that risk. I have affection for you, Dr. Lowell, deep affection. But I tell you that if my own mother tried to stop me in this I would sweep her aside as ruthlessly as I shall you.'

I said: 'I will go with you.'

'Then tell the nurse to bring me my clothing. Until all is over, we remain together. I am taking no more chances.'

I took up the telephone and gave the necessary order. McCann returned, and Ricori said to him:

'When I am clothed, we go to the doll-shop. Who is in the car with Tony?'

'Larson and Cartello.'

'Good. It may be that the witch knows we are coming. It may be that she has listened through the girl's dead ears as she spoke from her dead throat. No matter. We shall assume that she did not. Are there bars on the door?'

McCann said: 'Boss, I ain't been in the shop. I don't know. There's a glass panel. If there's bars we can work 'em. Tony'll get the tools while you put on your clothes.'

'Dr. Lowell,' Ricori turned on me. 'Will you give me your word that you will not change your mind about going with me? Nor attempt to interfere in what I am going to do?'

'I give you my word, Ricori.'

'McCann, you need not come back. Wait for us in the car.'

Ricori was soon dressed. As I walked with him out of my house, a clock struck one. I remembered that this strange adventure had begun, weeks ago, at that very hour. . . .

I rode in the back of the car with Ricori, the dead girl between us. On the middle seats were Larson and Cartello, the former a stolid Swede, the latter a wiry little Italian. The man named Tony drove, McCann beside him. We swung down the avenue and in about half an hour were on lower Broadway. As we drew near the street of the doll-maker, we went less quickly. The sky was overcast, a cold wind blowing off the bay. I shivered, but not with cold.

We came to the corner of the doll-maker's street.

For several blocks we had met no one, seen no one. It was as though we were passing through a city of the dead. Equally deserted was the street of the doll-maker.

Ricori said to Tony:

'Draw up opposite the doll-shop. We'll get out. Then go down to the corner. Wait for us there.'

My heart was beating uncomfortably. There was a quality of blackness in the night that seemed to swallow up the glow from the street lamps. There was no light in the doll-maker's shop, and in the old-fashioned doorway, set level with the street, the shadows clustered. The wind whined, and I could hear the beating of waves on the Battery wall. I wondered whether I would be able to go through that doorway, or whether the inhibition the doll-maker had put upon me still held me.

McCann slipped out of the car, carrying the girl's body. He propped her, sitting in the doorway's shadows. Ricori and I, Larson and Cartello, followed. The car rolled off. And again I felt the sense of nightmare unreality which had clung to me so often since I had first set my feet on this strange path to the doll-maker. . . .

The little Italian was smearing the glass of the door with some gummy material. In the center of it he fixed a small vacuum cup of rubber. He took a tool from his pocket and drew with it a foot-wide circle on the glass. The point of the tool cut into the glass as though it had been wax. Holding the vacuum cup in one hand, he tapped the glass lightly with a rubber-tipped hammer. The circle of glass came away in his hand. All had been done without the least sound. He reached through the

188

hole, and fumbled about noiselessly for a few moments. There was a faint click. The door swung open.

McCann picked up the dead girl. We went, silent as phantoms, into the doll-shop. The little Italian set the circle of glass back in its place. I could see dimly the door that opened into the corridor leading to that evil room at the rear. The little Italian tried the knob. The door was locked. He worked for a few seconds, and the door swung open. Ricori leading, McCann behind him with the girl, we passed like shadows through the corridor and paused at the further door—

The door swung open before the little Italian could touch it.

We heard the voice of the doll-maker!

'Enter, gentlemen. It was thoughtful of you to bring me back my dear niece! I would have met you at my outer door – but I am an old, old woman and timid!'

McCann whispered: 'One side, boss!'

He shifted the body of the girl to his left arm, and holding her like a shield, pistol drawn, began to edge by Ricori. Ricori thrust him away. His own automatic leveled, he stepped over the threshold. I followed McCann, the two gunmen at my back.

I took a swift glance around the room. The doll-maker sat at her table, sewing. She was serene, apparently untroubled. Her long white fingers danced to the rhythm of her stitches. She did not look up at us. There were coals burning in the fireplace. The room was very warm, and there was a strong aromatic odor, unfamiliar to me. I looked toward the cabinets of the dolls.

Every cabinet was open. Dolls stood within them, row upon row, staring down at us with eyes green and blue, gray and black, lifelike as though they were midgets on exhibition in some grotesque peep-show.

There must have been hundreds of them. Some were dressed as we in America dress; some as the Germans do; some as the Spanish, the French, the English; others were in costumes I did not recognize. A ballerina, and a blacksmith with his hammer raised . . . a French chevalier, and a German student, broadsword in hand, livid scars upon his face . . . an Apache with knife in hand, drug-madness on his yellow face and next to him a vicious-mouthed woman of the streets and next to her a jockey. . . .

The loot of the doll-maker from a dozen lands!

The dolls seemed to be poised to leap. To flow down upon us. Overwhelm us.

I steadied my thoughts. I forced myself to meet that battery of living dolls' eyes as though they were but lifeless dolls. There was an empty cabinet . . . another and another . . . five cabinets without dolls. The four dolls I had watched march upon me in the paralysis of the green glow were not there . . . nor was Walters. . . .

I wrenched my gaze away from the tiers of the watching dolls. I looked again at the doll-maker, still placidly sewing . . . as though she were alone . . . as though she were unaware of us . . . as though Ricori's pistol were not pointed at her heart . . . sewing . . . singing softly. . . .

The Walters doll was on the table before her!

It lay prone on its back. Its tiny hands were fettered at the wrists with twisted cords of the ashen hair. They were bound round and round, and the fettered hands clutched the hilt of a dagger-pin!

Long in the telling, but brief in the seeing – a few seconds in time as we measure it.

The doll-maker's absorption in her sewing, her utter indifference to us, the silence, made a screen between

190

us and her, an ever-thickening though invisible barrier. The pungent aromatic fragrance grew stronger.

McCann dropped the body of the girl on the floor. He tried to speak – once, twice; at the third attempt he succeeded. He said to Ricori hoarsely, in strangled voice:

'Kill her . . . or I will—'

Ricori did not move. He stood rigid, automatic pointed at the doll-maker's heart, eyes fixed on her dancing hands. He did not seem to hear McCann, or if he heard, he did not heed. The doll-maker's song went on . . . it was like the hum of bees . . . it was a sweet droning . . . it garnered sleep as the bees garner honey . . . sleep. . . .

Ricori shifted his grip upon his gun. He sprang forward. He swung the butt of the pistol down upon a wrist of the doll-maker.

The hand dropped, the fingers of that hand writhed . . . hideously the long white fingers writhed and twisted . . . like serpents whose backs have been broken. . . .

Ricori raised the gun for a second blow. Before it could fall the doll-maker had leaped to her feet, overturning her chair. A whispering ran over the cabinets like a thin veil of sound. The dolls seemed to bend, to lean forward. . . .

The doll-maker's eyes were on us now. They seemed to take in each and all of us at once. And they were like flaming black suns in which danced tiny crimson flames.

Her will swept out and overwhelmed us. It was like a wave, tangible. I felt it strike me as though it were a material thing. A numbness began to creep through me. I saw the hand of Ricori that clutched the pistol twitch and whiten. I knew that same numbness was gripping him . . . as it gripped McCann and the others. . . .

191

Once more the doll-maker had trapped us!

I whispered: 'Don't look at her, Ricori . . . don't look in her eyes. . . .'

With a tearing effort I wrested my own away from those flaming black ones. They fell upon the Walters doll. Stiffly, I reached to take it up – why, I did not know. The doll-maker was quicker than I. She snatched up the doll with her uninjured hand, and held it to her breast. She cried, in a voice whose vibrant sweetness ran through every nerve, augmenting the creeping lethargy:

'You will not look at me? You will not look at me! Fools – you can do nothing else!'

Then began that strange, that utterly strange episode that was the beginning of the end.

The aromatic fragrance seemed to pulse, to throb, grow stronger. Something like a sparkling mist whirled out of nothingness and covered the doll-maker, veiling the horselike face, the ponderous body. Only her eyes shone through that mist. . . .

The mist cleared away. Before us stood a woman of breath-taking beauty – tall and slender and exquisite. Naked, her hair, black and silken fine, half-clothed her to her knees. Through it the pale golden flesh gleamed. Only the eyes, the hands, the doll still clasped to one of the round, high breasts told who she was.

Ricori's automatic dropped from his hand. I heard the weapons of the others fall to the floor. I knew they stood rigid as I, stunned by that incredible transformation, and helpless in the grip of the power streaming from the doll-maker.

She pointed to Ricori and laughed: 'You would kill me – *me*! Pick up your weapon, Ricori – and try!'

Ricori's body bent slowly . . . slowly . . . I could see

him only indirectly, for my eyes could not leave the woman's . . . and I knew that his could not . . . that, fastened to them, his eyes were turning upward, upward as he bent. I sensed rather than saw that his groping hand had touched his pistol – that he was trying to lift it. I heard him groan. The doll-maker laughed again.

'Enough, Ricori – you cannot!'

Ricori's body straightened with a snap, as though a hand clutched his chin and thrust him up. . . .

There was a rustling behind me, the patter of little feet, the scurrying of small bodies past me.

At the feet of the women were four mannikins . . . the four who had marched upon me in the green glow . . . banker-doll, spinster-doll, the acrobat, the trapeze performer.

They stood, the four of them, ranged in front of her, glaring at us. In the hand of each was a dagger-pin, points thrust at us like tiny swords. And once more the laughter of the woman filled the room. She spoke, caressingly:

'No, no, my little ones. I do not need you!'

She pointed to me.

'You know this body of mine is but illusion, do you not? Speak?'

'Yes.'

'And these at my feet – and all my little ones – are but illusions?'

I said: 'I do not know that.'

'You know too much – and you know too little. Therefore you must die, my too wise and too foolish doctor—' The great eyes dwelt upon me with mocking pity, the lovely face became maliciously pitiful. 'And Ricori too must die – because he knows too much. And you others – you too must die. But not at the hands of

193

my little people. Not here. No! At your home, my good doctor. You shall go there silently – speaking neither among yourselves nor to any others on your way. And when there – you will turn upon yourselves . . . each slaying the other . . . rending yourselves like wolves . . . like—'

She staggered back a step, reeling.

I saw – or thought I saw – the doll of Walters writhe. Then swift as a striking snake it raised its bound hands and thrust the dagger-pin through the doll-maker's throat . . . twisted it savagely . . . and thrust and thrust again . . . stabbing the golden throat of the woman precisely where that other doll had stabbed Braile!

And as Braile had screamed – so now screamed the doll-maker . . . dreadfully, agonizedly. . . .

She tore the doll from her breast. She hurled it from her. The doll hurtled toward the fireplace, rolled, and touched the glowing coals.

There was a flash of brilliant flame, a wave of that same intense heat I had felt when the match of McCann had struck the Peters doll. And instantly, at the touch of that heat, the dolls at the woman's feet vanished. From them arose swiftly a pillar of that same brilliant flame. It coiled and wrapped itself around the doll-maker, from feet to head.

I saw the shape of beauty melt away. In its place was the horse-like face, the immense body of Madame Mandilip . . . eyes seared and blind . . . the long white hands clutching at her torn throat, and no longer white but crimson with her blood.

Thus for an instant she stood, then toppled to the floor.

And at that instant of her fall, the spell that held us broke.

Ricori leaned toward the huddled hulk that had been the doll-maker. He spat upon it. He shouted, exultantly:

'Burn witch burn!'

He pushed me to the door, pointing toward the tiers of the watching dolls that strangely now seemed – lifeless! Only – dolls!

Fire was leaping to them from draperies and curtains. The fire was leaping at them as though it were some vengeful spirit of cleansing flame!

We rushed through the door, the corridor, out into the shop. Through the corridor and into the shop the flames poured after us. We ran into the street.

Ricori cried: 'Quick! To the car!'

Suddenly the street was red with the light of the flames. I heard windows opening, and shouts of warning and alarm.

We swung into the waiting car, and it leaped away.

CHAPTER EIGHTEEN

The Dark Wisdom

'They have made effigies comparable with my image,
similar to my form, who have taken away my breath,
pulled out my hair, torn my garments, prevented my
feet from moving by means of dust; with an ointment
of harmful herbs they rubbed me; to my death they
have led me – O God of Fire destroy them!'

Three weeks had passed since the death of the doll-maker. Ricori and I sat at dinner in my home. A silence had fallen between us. I had broken it with the curious invocation that begins this, the concluding chapter of my narrative, scarcely aware that I had spoken aloud. But Ricori looked up, sharply.

'You quote someone? Whom?'

I answered: 'A tablet of clay, inscribed by some Chaldean in the days of Assur-nizir-pal, three thousand years ago.'

He said: 'And in those few words he has told all our story!'

'Even so, Ricori. It is all there – the dolls – the unguent – the torture – death – and the cleansing flame.'

He mused: 'It is strange, that. Three thousand years ago – and even then they knew the evil and its remedy ... "effigies similar to my form ... who have taken away my breath ... an ointment of harmful herbs ... to my death they have led me ... O God of Fire – destroy them!" *Si*, it is all our story, Dr. Lowell.'

I said: 'The death-dolls are far, far older than Ur of

196

the Chaldees. Older than history. I have followed their trail down the ages since the night Braile was killed. And it is a long, long trail, Ricori. They have been found buried deep in the hearths of the Cro-Magnons, hearths whose fires died twenty thousand years ago. And they have been found under still colder hearths of still more ancient peoples. Dolls of flint, dolls of stone, dolls carved from the mammoth's tusks, from the bones of the cave bear, from the saber-toothed tiger's fangs. They had the dark wisdom even then, Ricori.'

He nodded: 'Once I had a man about me whom I liked well. A Transylvanian. One day I asked him why he had come to America. He told me a strange tale. He said that there had been a girl in his village whose mother, so it was whispered, knew things no Christian should know. He put it thus, cautiously, crossing himself. The girl was comely, desirable – yet he could not love her. She, it seemed, loved him – or perhaps it was his indifference that drew her. One afternoon, coming home from the hunt, he passed her hut. She called to him. He was thirsty, and drank the wine she offered him. It was good wine. It made him gay – but it did not make him love her.

'Nevertheless, he went with her into the hut, and drank more wine. Laughing, he let her cut hair from his head, pare his finger-nails, take drops of blood from his wrist, and spittle from his mouth. Laughing, he left her, and went home, and slept. When he awakened, it was early evening, and all that he remembered was that he had drunk wine with the girl, but that was all.

'Something told him to go to church. He went to church. And as he knelt, praying, suddenly he did remember more – remembered that the girl had taken his hair, his nail parings, his spittle and his blood. And he felt a great necessity to go to this girl and to see what she was doing with his hair, his nail parings, his spittle, his blood. It was as though he said, the Saint before whom he knelt was commanding him to do this.

'So he stole to the hut of the girl, slipped through the wood, creeping up to her window. He looked in. She sat at the hearth, kneading dough as though for bread. He was ashamed that he had crept so with such thoughts – but then he saw that into the dough she was dropping the hair she had cut from him, the nail parings, the blood, the spittle. She was kneading them within the dough. Then, as he watched, he saw her take the dough and model it into the shape of a little man. And she sprinkled water upon its head, baptizing it in his name with strange words he could not understand.

'He was frightened, this man. But also he was greatly enraged, Also he had courage. He watched until she had finished. He saw her wrap the doll in her apron, and come to the door. She went out of the door, and away. He followed her – he had been a woodsman and knew how to go softly, and she did not know he was following her. She came to a crossroads. There was a new moon shining, and some prayer she made to this new moon. Then she dug a hole, and placed the doll of dough in that hole. And then she defiled it. After this she said:

' "Zaru (it was this man's name! Zaru! Zaru! I love you. When this image is rotted away you must run after me as the dog after the bitch. You are mine, Zaru, soul and body. As the image rots, you become mine. When the image is rotted, you are all mine. Forever and forever and forever!"

'She covered the image with earth. He leaped upon her, and strangled her. He would have dug up the image, but he heard voices and was more afraid and ran. He did not go back to the village. He made his way to America.

'He told me that when he was out a day on that journey, he felt hands clutching at his loins – dragging him to the rail, to the sea. Back to the village, to the girl. By that, he knew he had not killed her. He fought the hands. Night after night he fought them. He dared not sleep, for when he slept he dreamed he was there at the cross-roads, the girl beside him – and three times he awakened just in time to check himself from throwing himself into the sea.

'Then the strength of the hands began to weaken. And at last, but not for many months, he felt them no more. But still he went, always afraid, until word came to him from the village. He had been right – he had not killed her. But later – someone else did. That girl had what you have named the dark wisdom. *Si!* Perhaps it turned against her at the end – as in the end it turned against the witch we knew.'

I said: 'It is curious that you should say that, Ricori . . . strange that you should speak of the dark wisdom turning against the one who commands it . . . but of that I will speak later. Love and hate and power – three lusts – always these seem to have been the three legs of the tripod on which burns the dark flame; the supports of the stage from which the death-dolls leap. . . .

'Do you know who is the first recorded Maker of Dolls? No? Well, he was a God, Ricori. His name was Khnum. He was a God long and long before Yawvah of the Jews, who was also a maker of dolls, you will recall, shaping two of them in the Garden of Eden; animating them; but giving them only two inalienable rights – first, the right to suffer; second, the right to die. Khnum was a far more merciful God. He did not deny the right to die – but he did not think the dolls should suffer; he liked to see them enjoy themselves in their brief breathing space. Khnum was so old that he had ruled in Egypt ages before the Pyramids or the Sphinx were thought of. He had a brother God whose name was Kepher, and who had the head of a Beetle. It was Kepher who sent a thought rippling like a little wind over the surface of Chaos. That thought fertilized Chaos, and from it the world was born. . . .

'Only a ripple over the surface, Ricori! If it had pierced the skin of Chaos . . . or thrust even deeper . . . into its heart . . . what might not mankind now be? Nevertheless, rippling, the thought achieved the superficiality that is man. The work of Khnum thereafter was to reach into the wombs of women and shape the body of the child who lay within. They called him the Potter-God. He it was who, at the command of Amen, greatest of the younger Gods, shaped the body of the great Queen Hat-shep-sut whom Amen begot, lying beside her mother in the likeness of the Pharaoh, her husband. At least, so wrote the priests of her day.

'But a thousand years before this there was a Prince whom Osiris and Isis loved greatly – for his beauty, his courage and his strength. Nowhere on earth, they thought, was there a woman fit for him. So they called Khnum, the Potter-God, to make one. He came, with long hands like those of . . . Madame Mandilip . . . like hers, each finger alive. He shaped the clay into a woman so beautiful that even the Goddess Isis felt a touch of envy. These were severely practical Gods, those of old Egypt, so they threw the Prince into a sleep, placed the woman beside him, and compared – the word in the ancient papyrus is "fitted" – them. Alas! She was not harmonious. She was too small. So Khnum made an-

200

other doll. But his was too large. And not until six were shaped and destroyed was true harmony attained, the Gods satisfied, the fortunate Prince given his perfect wife – who had been a doll.

'Ages after, in the time of Rameses III, it happened that there was a man who sought for and who found this secret of Khnum, the Potter-God. He had spent his whole life in seeking it. He was old and bent and withered; but the desire for women was still strong within him. All that he knew to do with that secret of Khnum was to satisfy that desire. But he felt the necessity of a model. Who were the fairest of women whom he could use as models? The wives of the Pharaoh, of course. So this man made certain dolls in the shape and semblance of those who accompanied the Pharaoh when he visited his wives. Also, he made a doll in the likeness of the Pharaoh himself; and into this he entered, animating it. His dolls then carried him into the royal harem, past the guards, who believed even as did the wives of Pharaoh, that he was the true Pharaoh. And entertained him accordingly.

'But, as he was leaving, the true Pharaoh entered. That must have been quite a situation, Ricori – suddenly, miraculously, in his harem, the Pharaoh doubled! But Khnum, seeing what had happened, reached down from Heaven and touched the dolls, withdrawing their life. And they dropped to the floor, and were seen to be – only dolls.

'While where one Pharaoh had stood lay another doll – and crouched beside it a shivering and wrinkled old man!

'You can find the story, and a fairly detailed account of the trial that followed, in a papyrus of the time; now, I think, in the Turin Museum. Also a catalogue of the

201

tortures the magician underwent before he was burned. Now, there is no manner of doubt that there were such accusations, nor that there was such a trial; the papyrus is authentic. But what, actually, was at the back of it? Something happened – but what was it? Is the story only another record of superstition – or does it deal with the fruit of the dark wisdom?'

Ricori said: 'You, yourself, watched that dark wisdom fruit. Are you still unconvinced of its reality?'

I did not answer; I continued: 'The knotted cord – the Witch's Ladder. That, too, is most ancient. The oldest document of Frankish legislation, the Salic Law, reduced to written form about fifteen hundred years ago, provided the severest penalities for those who tied what it named the Witch's Knot—'

'*La ghirlanda della strega*,' he said. 'Well, do we know that cursed thing in my land – and to our black sorrow!'

I took startled note of his pallid face, his twitching fingers; I said, hastily: 'But of course, Ricori, you realize that all I have been quoting is legend? Folklore. With no proven basis of scientific fact.'

He thrust his chair back, violently, arose, stared at me, incredulously. He spoke, with effort: 'You still hold that the devil-work we witnessed can be explained in terms of the science you know?'

I stirred, uncomfortably: 'I did not say that, Ricori. I do say that Madame Mandilip was as extraordinary a hypnotist as she was a murderess – a mistress of illusion—'

He interrupted me, hands clenching the table's edge: 'You think her dolls were – illusions?'

I answered, obliquely: 'You know how real was that illusion of a beautiful body. Yet we saw it dissolve

in the true reality of the flames. It had seemed as verit-
able as the dolls, Ricori—'

Again he interrupted me: 'The stab in my heart . . .
the doll that killed Gilmore . . . the doll that murdered
Braile . . . the blessed doll that slew the witch! You call
them illusions?'

I answered, a little sullenly, the old incredulity suddenly strong within me: 'It is entirely possible that,
obeying a post-hypnotic command of the doll-maker,
you, yourself, thrust the dagger-pin into your own heart!
It is possible that obeying a similar command, given
when and where and how I do not know, Peters' sister,
herself, killed her husband. The chandelier fell on
Braile when I was, admittedly, under the influence of
those same post-hypnotic influences – and it is possible
that it was a sliver of glass that cut his carotid. As for
the doll-maker's own death, apparently at the hands
of the Walters doll – well, it is also possible that the
abnormal mind of Madame Mandilip was, at times,
the victim of the same illusions she induced in the minds
of others. The doll-maker was a mad genius, governed
by a morbid compulsion to surround herself with the
effigies of those she had killed by the unguent. Marguerite de Valois, Queen of Navarre, carried constantly
with her the embalmed hearts of a dozen or more lovers
who had died for her. She had not slain those men – but
she knew she had been the cause of their deaths as
surely as though she had strangled them with her own
hands. The psychological principle involved in Queen
Marguerite's collection of hearts and Madame Mandilip's collection of dolls is one and the same.'

He had not sat down; still in that strained voice he
repeated: 'I asked you if you called the killing of the
witch an illusion.'

I said: 'You make it very uncomfortable for me, Ricori – staring at me like that . . . and I am answering your question. I repeat it is possible that in her own mind she was at times the victim of the same illusions she induced in the minds of others. That at times she, herself, thought the dolls were alive. That in this strange mind was conceived a hatred for the doll of Walters. And, at the last, under the irritation of our attack, this belief reacted upon her. That thought was in my mind when, a while ago. I said it was curious that you should speak of the dark wisdom turning those who possessed it. She tormented the doll; she expected the doll to avenge itself if it had the opportunity. So strong was this belief, or expectation, that when the favorable moment arrived, she dramatized it. Her thought became action! The doll-maker, like you, may well have plunged the dagger-pin into her own throat—'

'*You fool!*'

The words came from Ricori's mouth – and yet it was so like Madame Mandilip speaking in her haunted room and speaking through the dead lips of Laschna that I dropped back into my chair, shuddering.

Ricori was leaning over the table. His black eyes were blank, expressionless. I cried out, sharply, a panic shaking me: 'Ricori – wake—'

The dreadful blankness in his eyes flicked away; their gaze sharpened, was intent upon me. He said, again in his own voice:

'I am awake, I am so awake – that I will listen to you no more! Instead – listen you to me, Dr. Lowell. I say to you – to hell with your science! I tell you this – that beyond the curtain of the material at which our vision halts, there are forces and energies that hate us, yet which God in his inscrutable wisdom permits to be.

I tell you that these powers can reach through the veil of matter and become manifest in creatures like the doll-maker. It is so! Witches and sorcerers hand in hand with evil! It is so! And there are powers friendly to us which make themselves manifest in their chosen ones.

'I say to you – Madame Mandilip was an accursed witch! An instrument of the evil powers! Whore of Satan! She burned as a witch should burn. She shall burn in hell – forever! I say to you that the little nurse was an instrument of the good powers. And she is happy to-day in Paradise – as she shall be forever!'

He was silent, trembling with his own fervor. He touched my shoulder:

'Tell me, Dr. Lowell – tell me as truthfully as though you stood before the seat of God, believing in Him as I believe – do those scientific explanations of yours truly satisfy you?'

I answered, very quietly:

'No, Ricori.'

Nor do they.